**Publisher's Cataloging-in-Publication**
*(Provided by Quality Books, Inc.)*

Messinger, Midge.
Freddie Q. Freckle / by Midge Messinger ; new illustrations by Margaret Ferraro-Oster ; edited by Robert M. Messinger. -- 1st ed.
p. cm.
SUMMARY : In a dream, a little girl named Susie meets a homeless freckle and offers him a home on her hand.
Preassigned LCCN: 98-92167
ISBN: 1-893237-00-1
1. Human skin color--Juvenile fiction. 2. Dreams--Juvenile fiction. 3. Homelessness--Juvenile fiction. I. Ferraro-Oster, Margaret. II. Messinger, Robert M. III. Title.

PZ8.3.M559275Fre 1998 [E]
QBI98-1411


Published by Little Mai Press, Inc., 102 River Drive, Lake Hiawatha, NJ 07034.
Library of Congress Catalog Number: 98-92167.
ISBN: 1-893237-00-1
Printed in Hong Kong.

# FREDDIE Q. FRECKLE

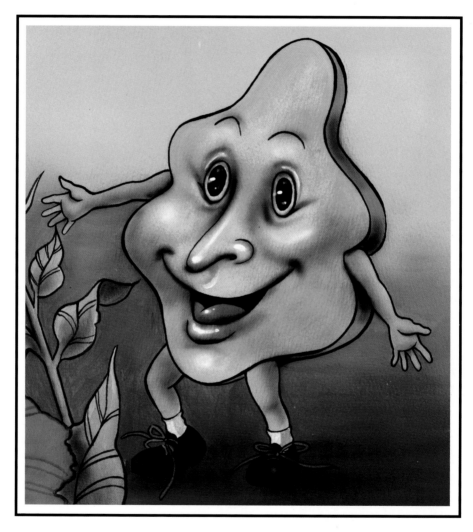

by Midge Messinger

**NEW ILLUSTRATIONS BY**
Margaret Ferraro-Oster

**EDITED BY**
Robert M. Messinger

Susie
woke
up one
morning, early
and bright.

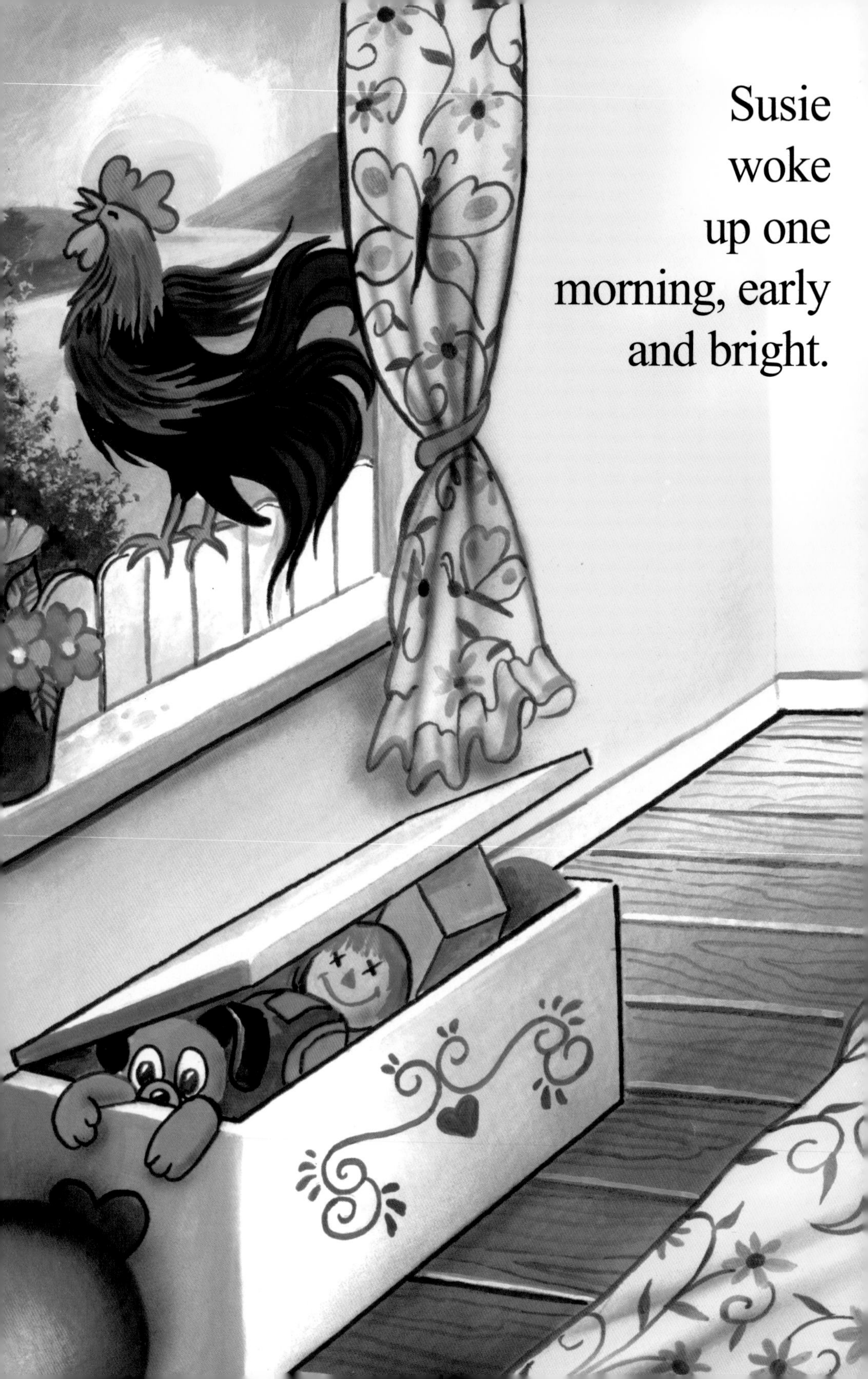

It seems that she had a wonderful night.

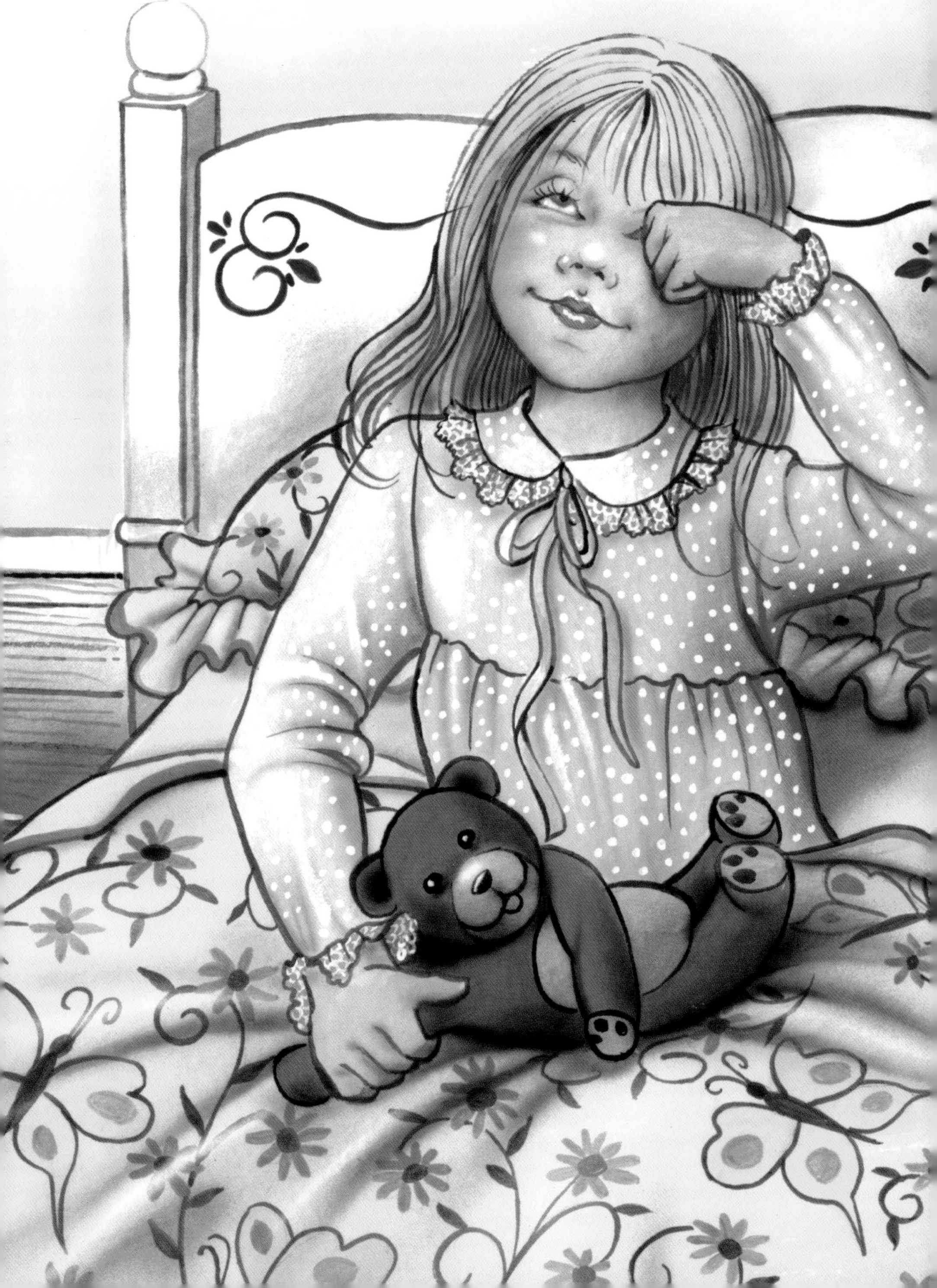

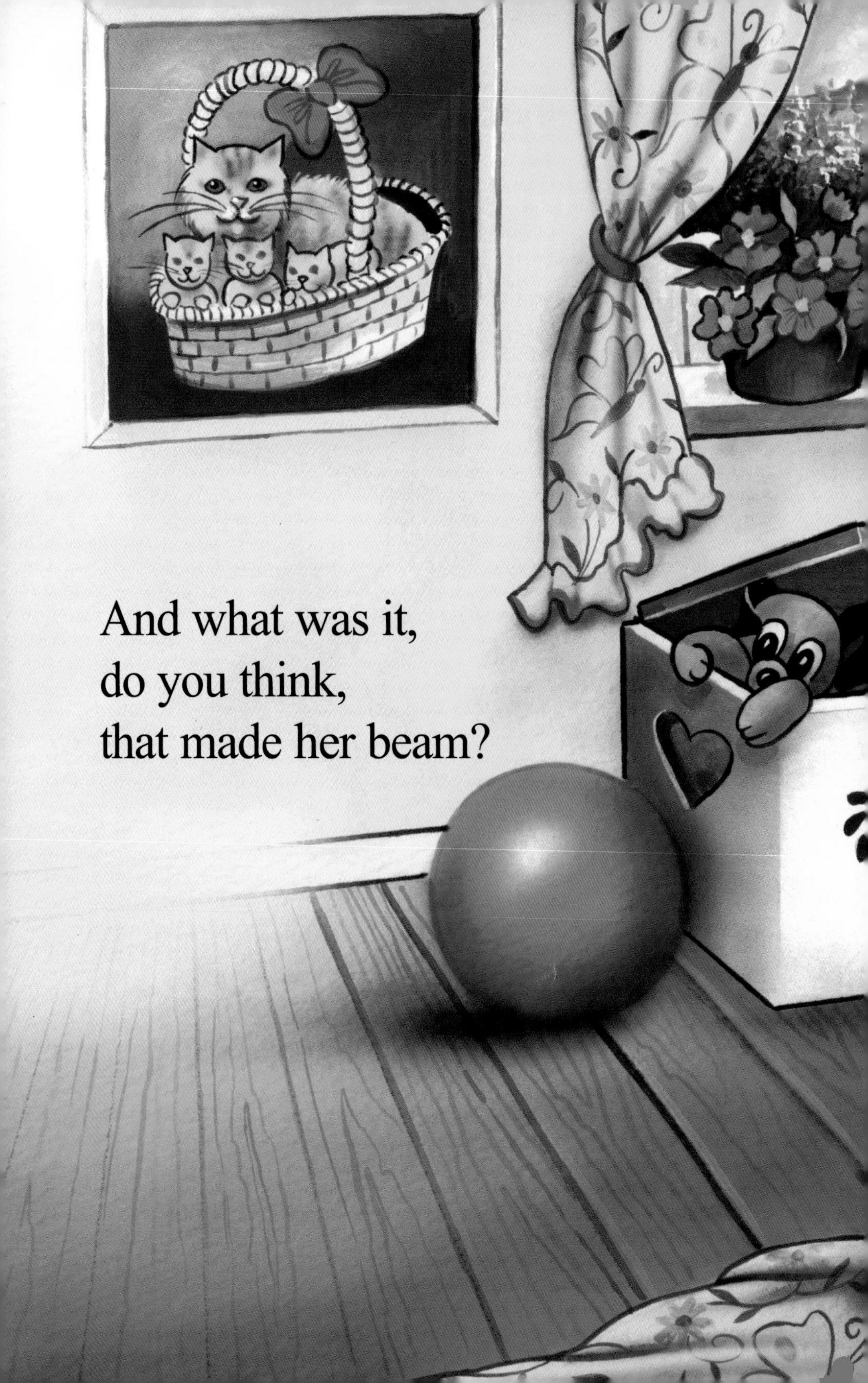

And what was it,
do you think,
that made her beam?

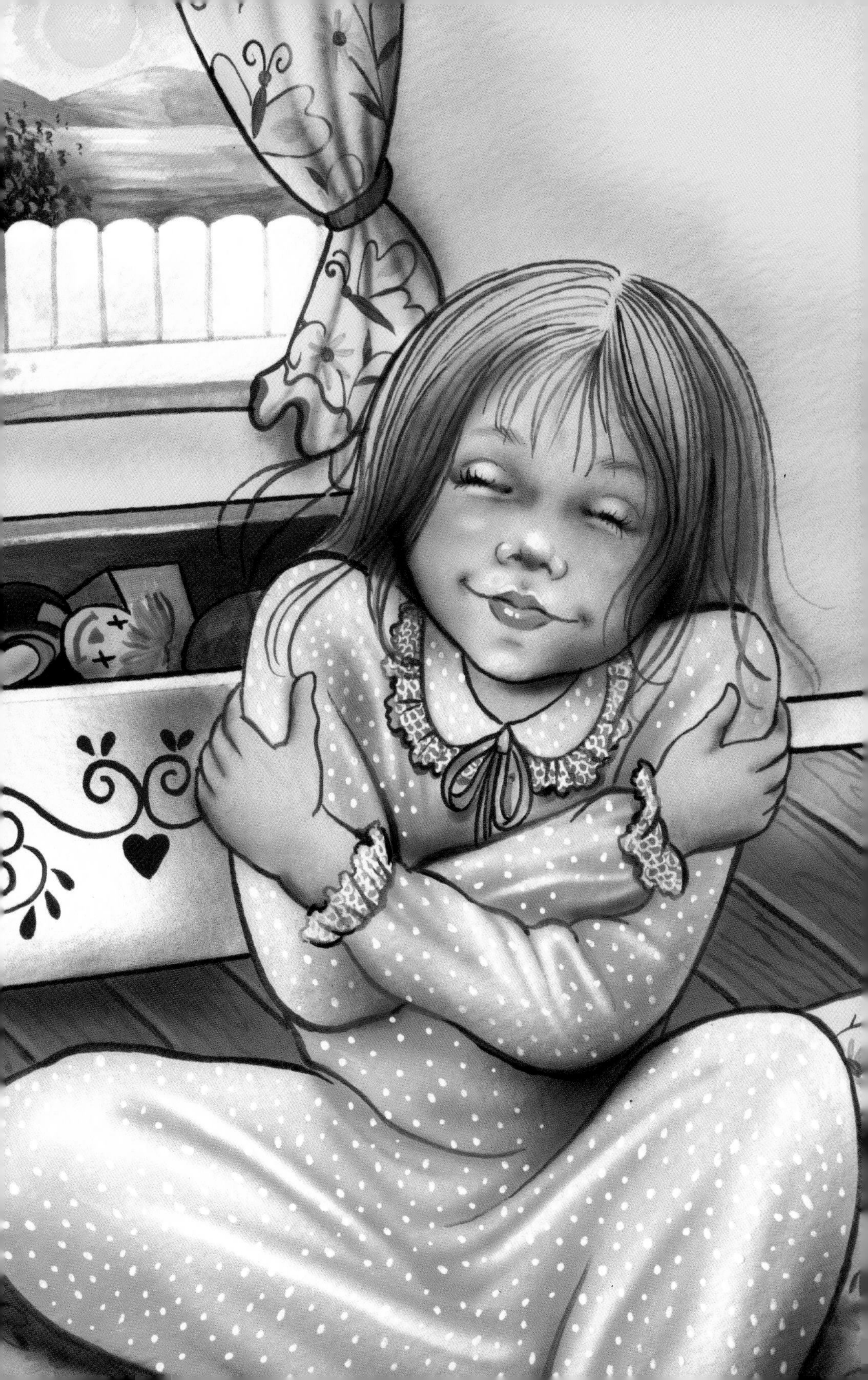

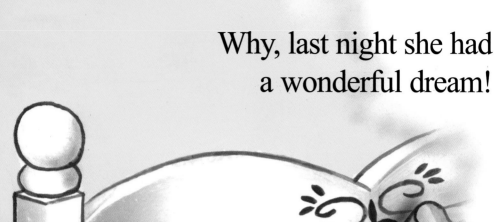

Why, last night she had
a wonderful dream!

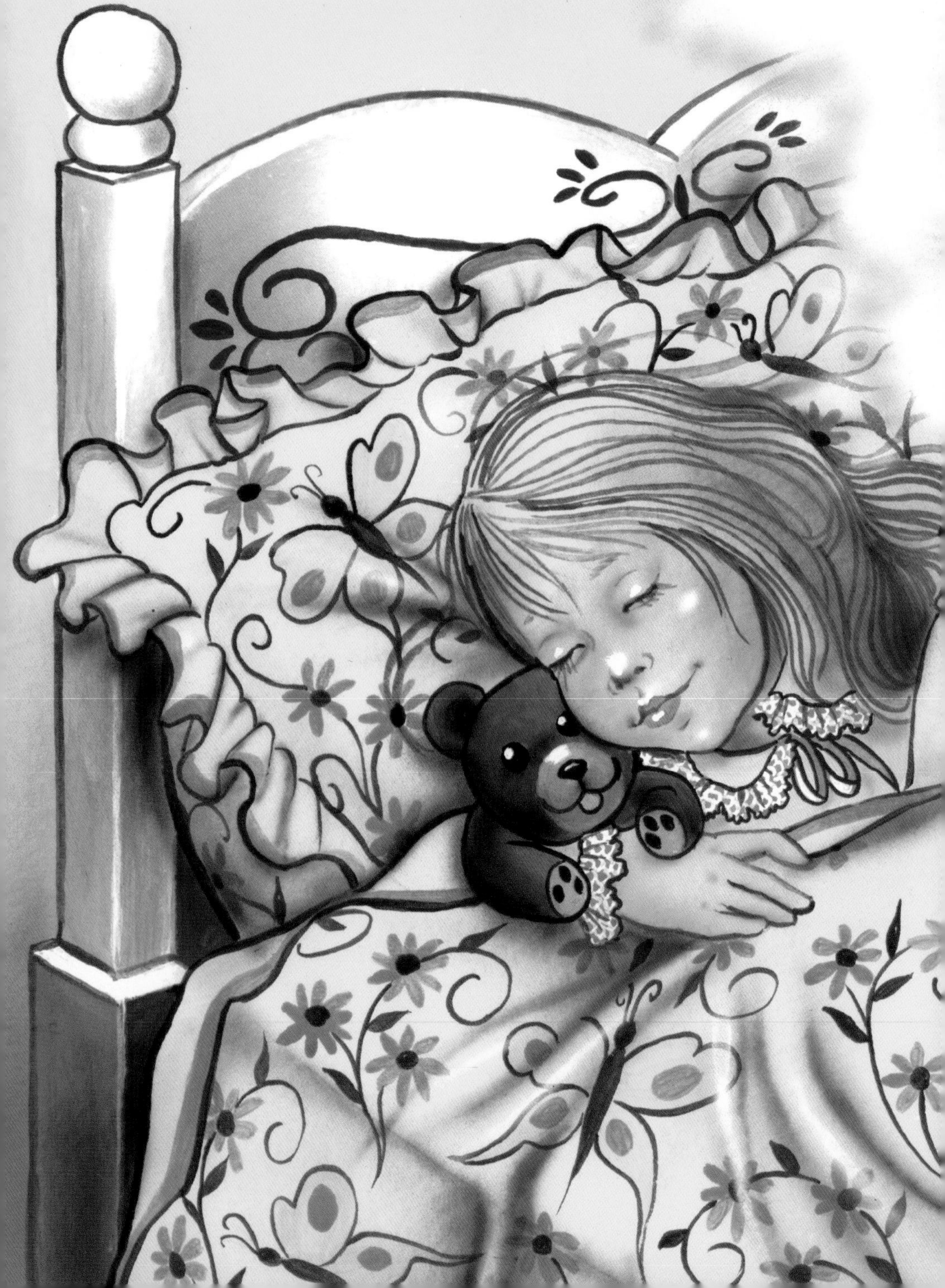

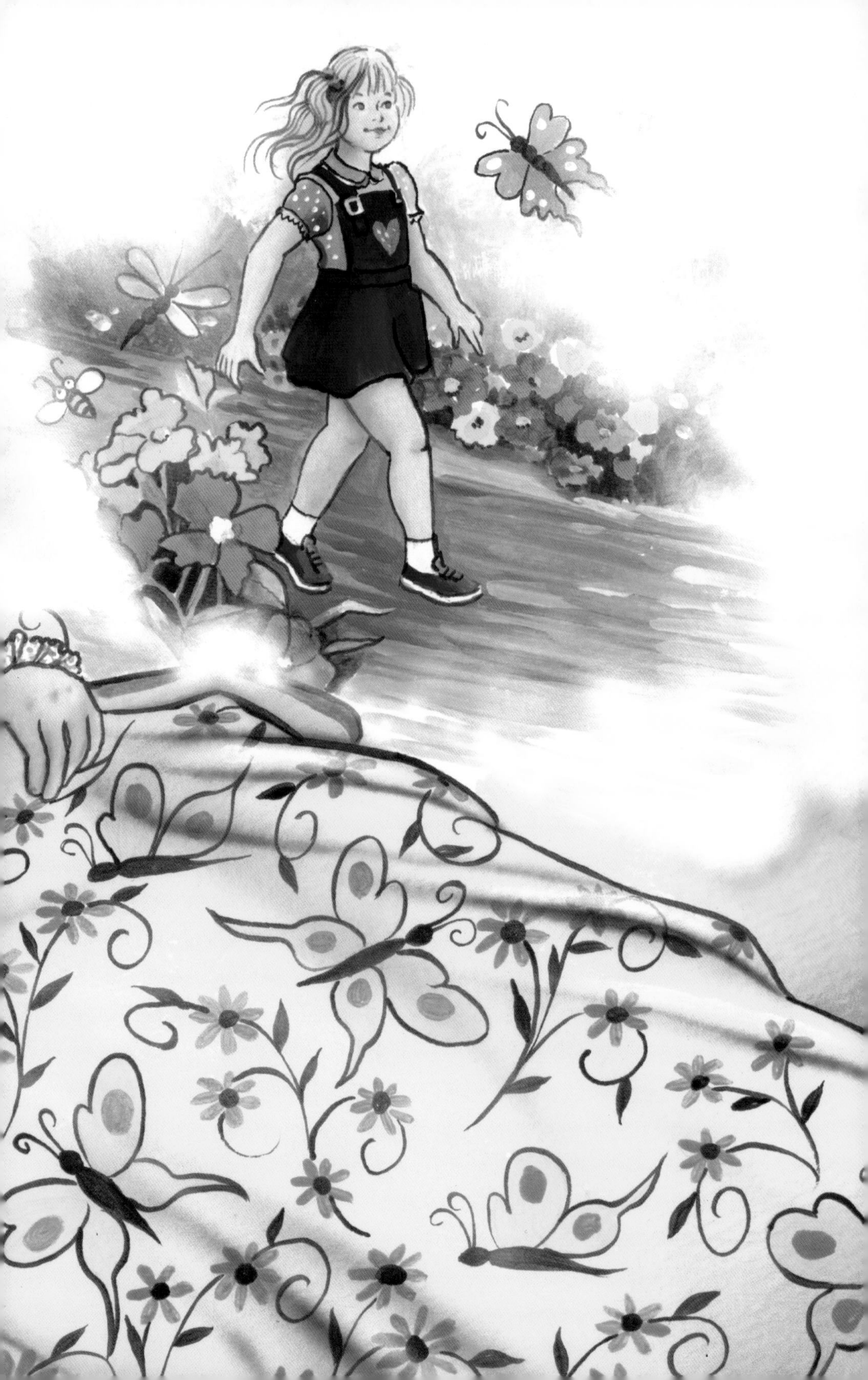

She dreamed that she
was walking along,
singing a pretty and
happy song.

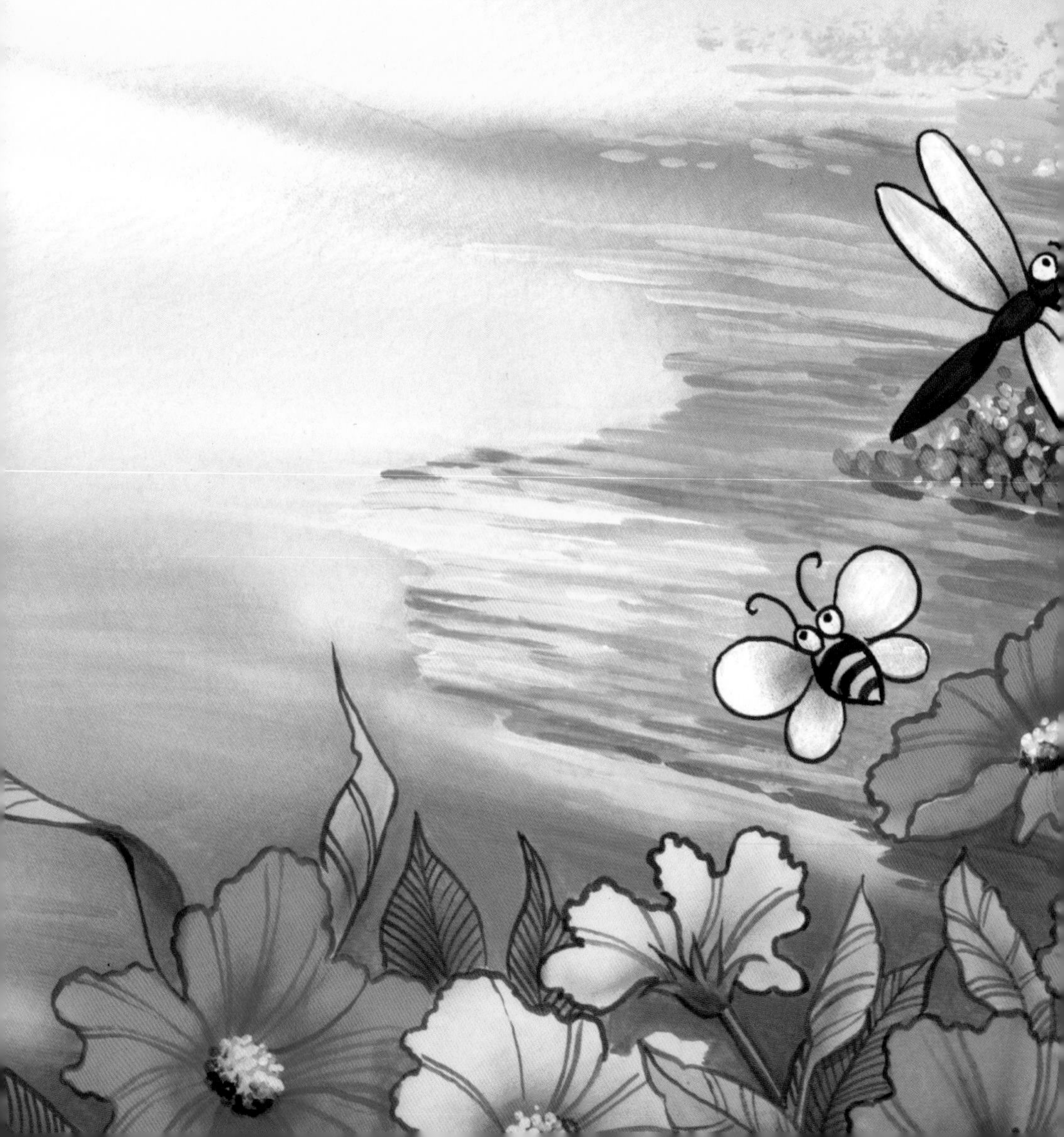

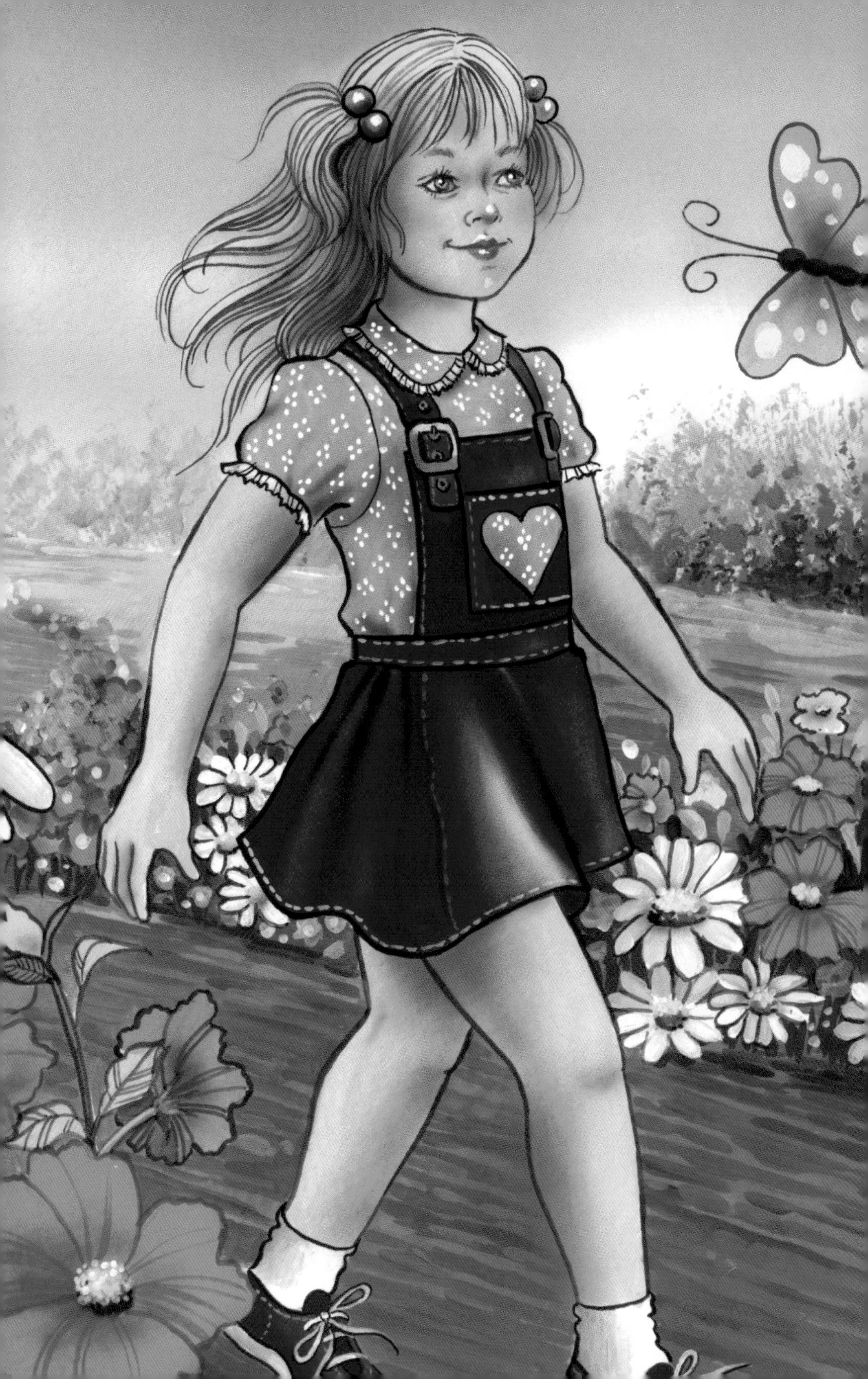

When all of a sudden,
from out of nowhere,
the sound of crying
came to her ear.

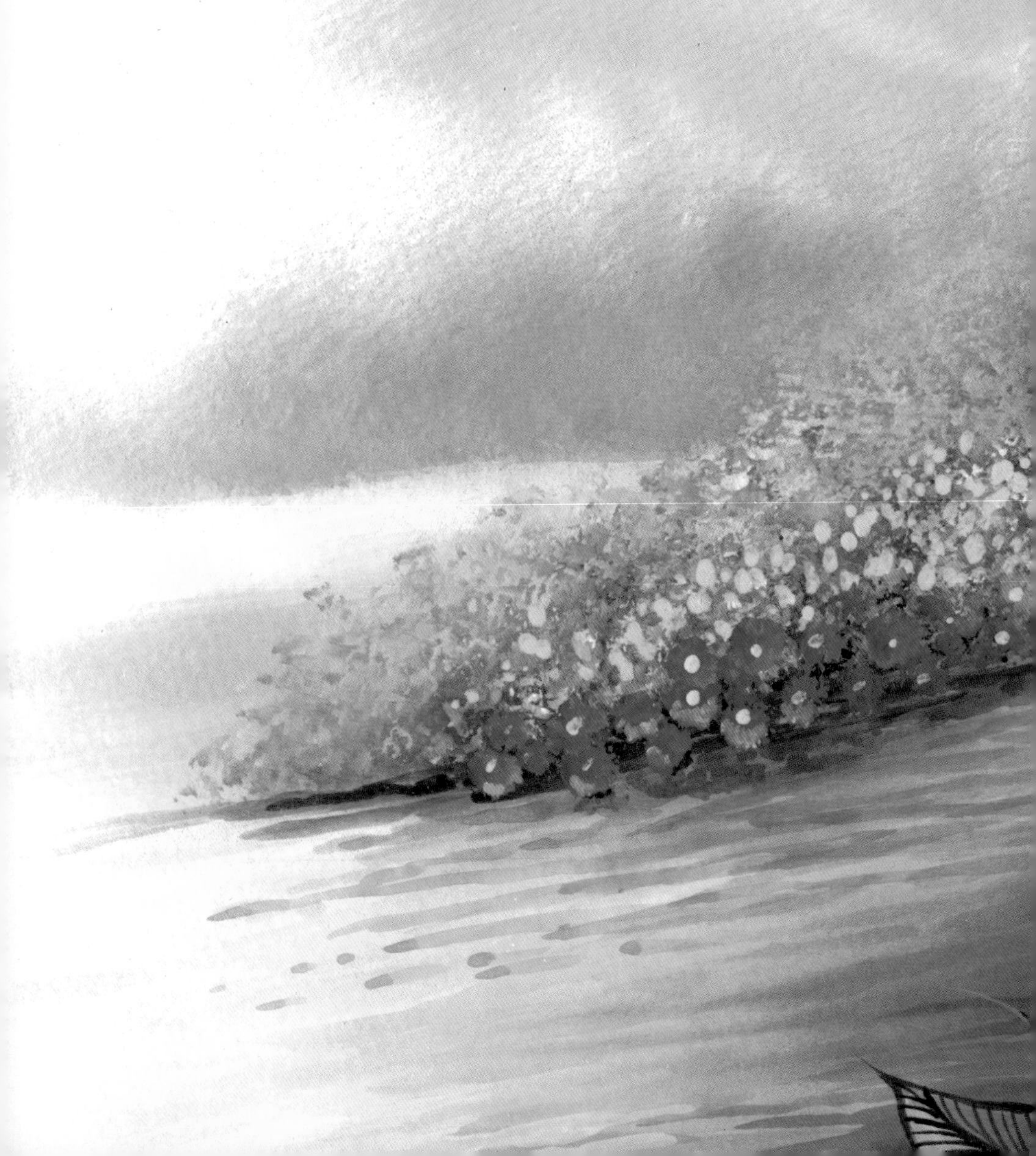

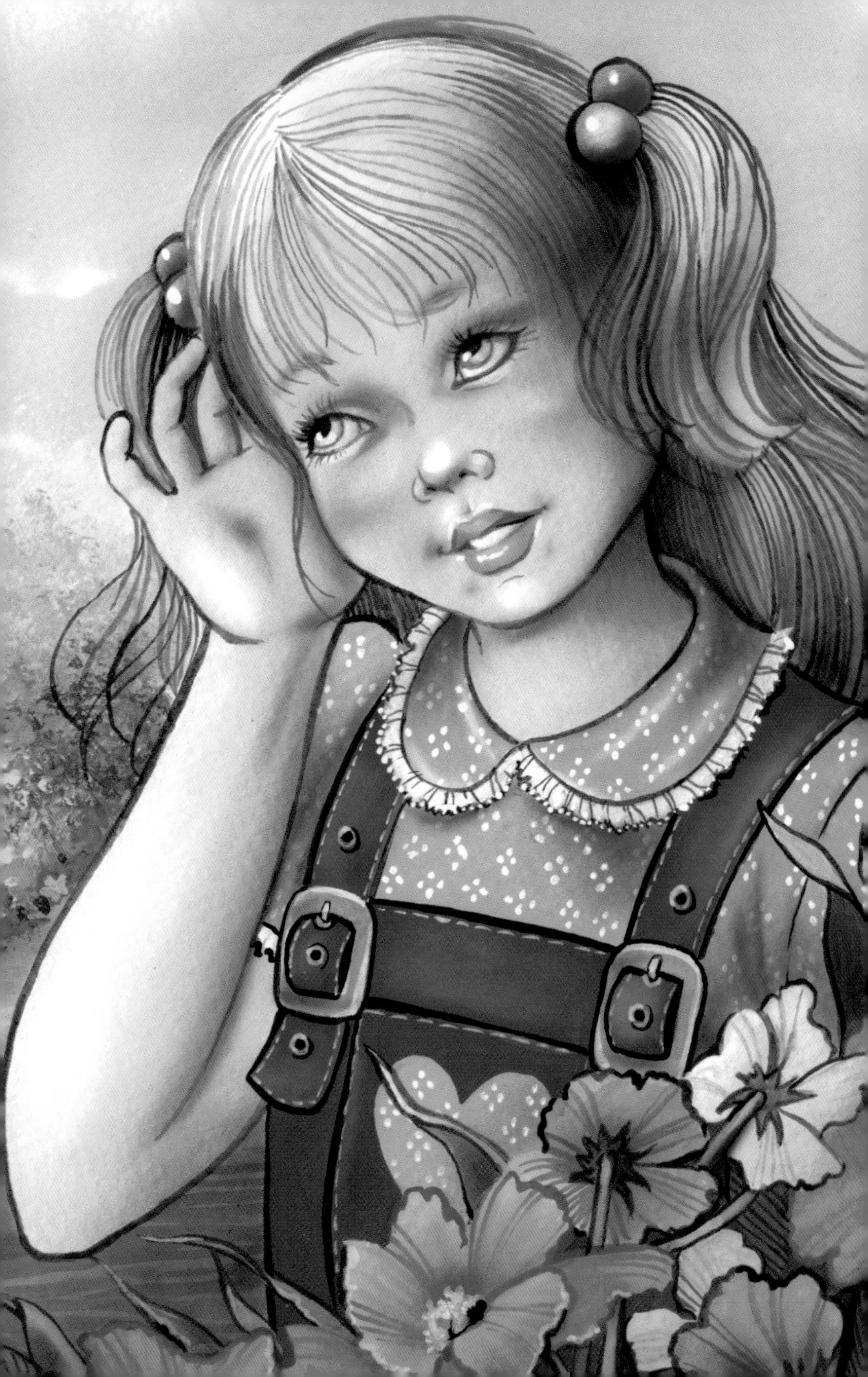

She looked up and down...

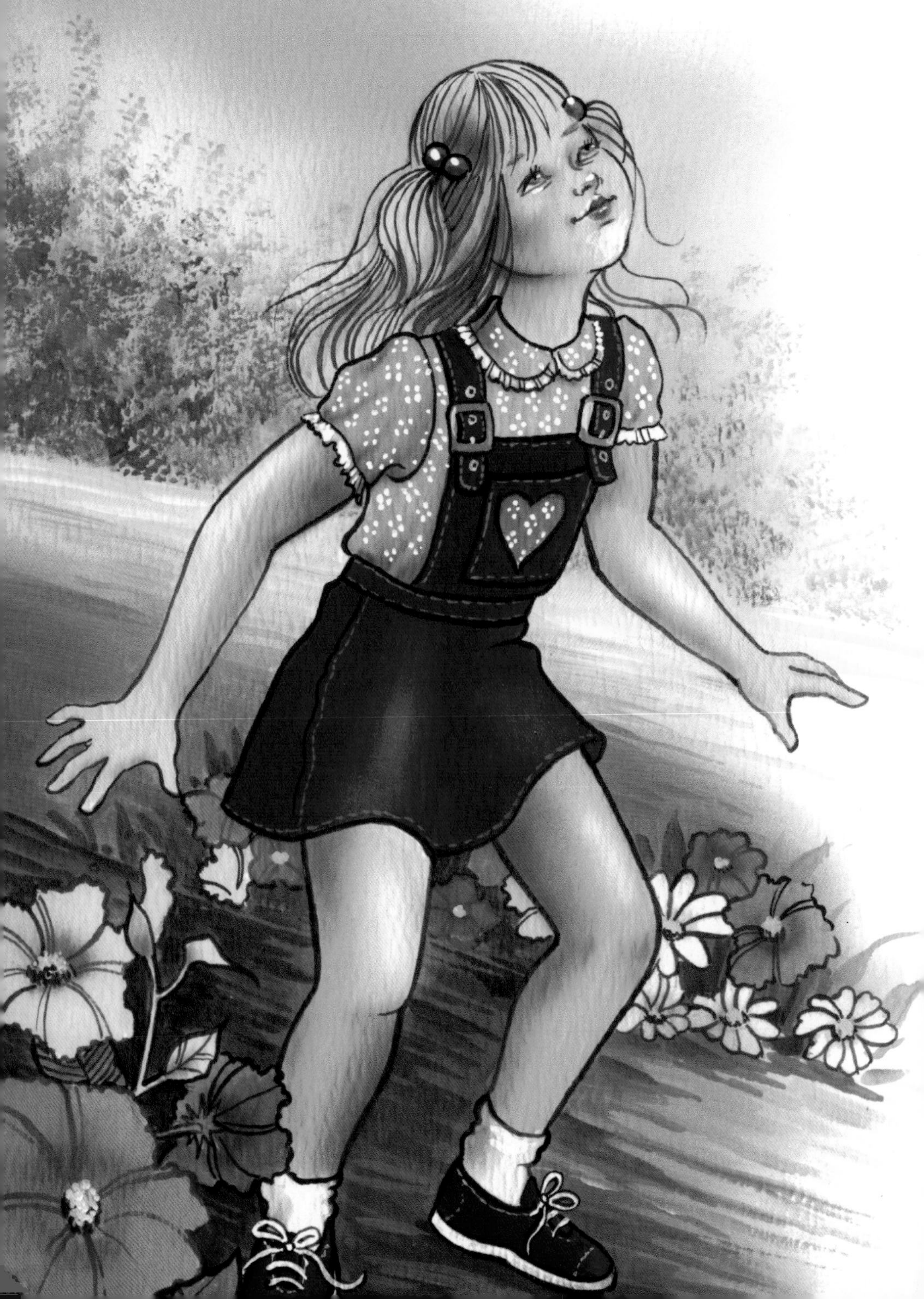

She looked all around...

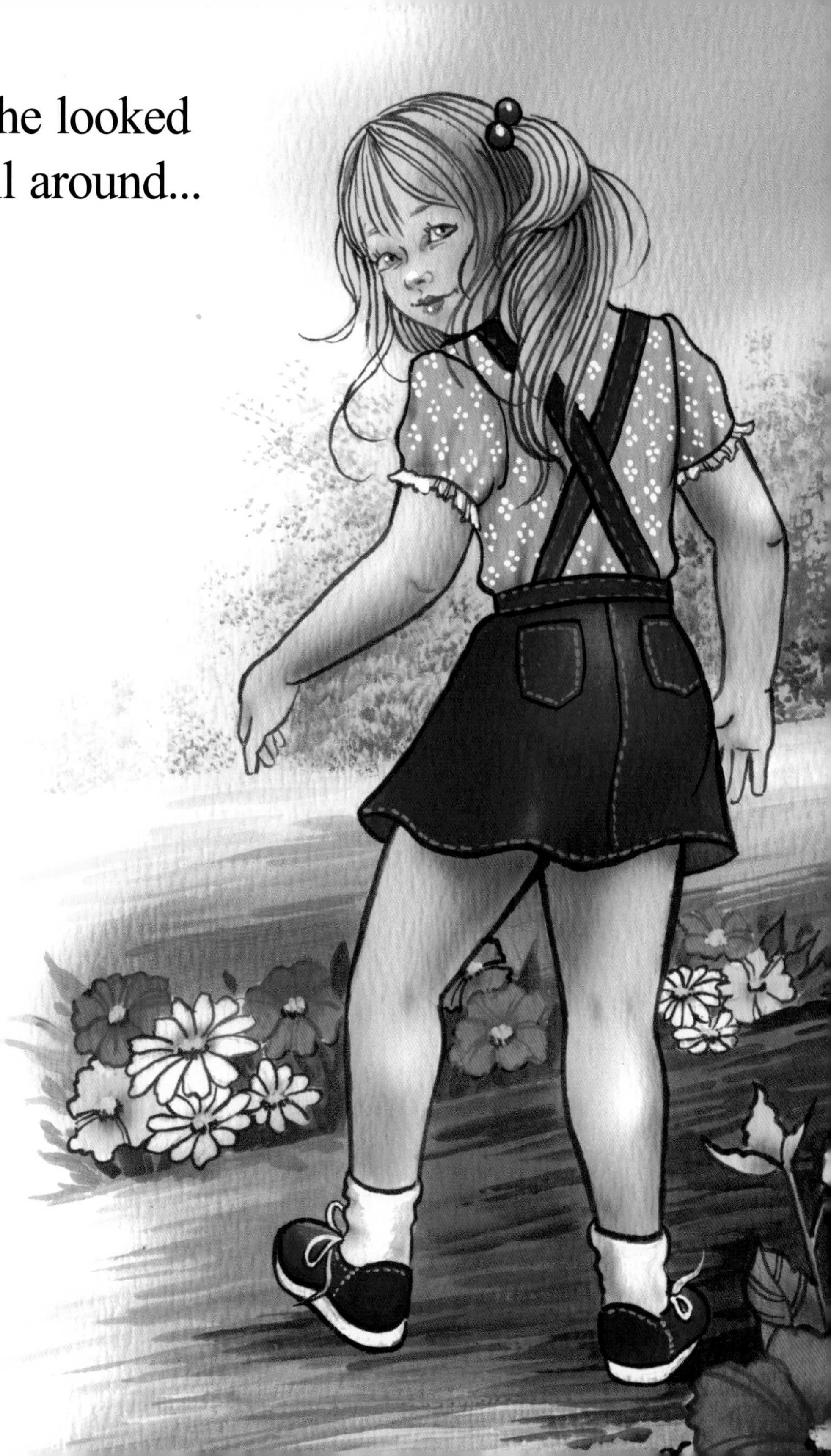

She looked
over and underneath.

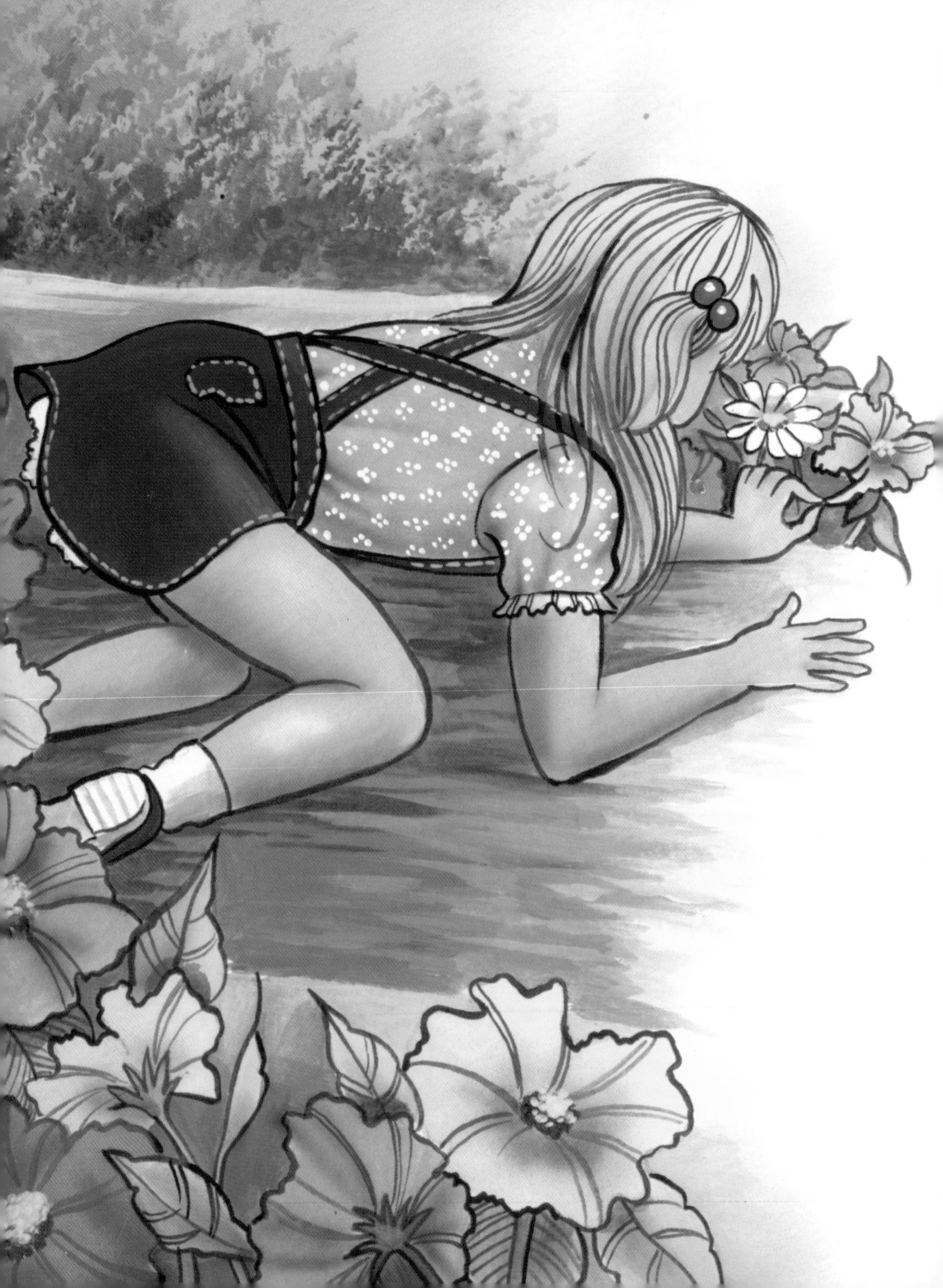

She looked up in the air,
she looked everywhere...

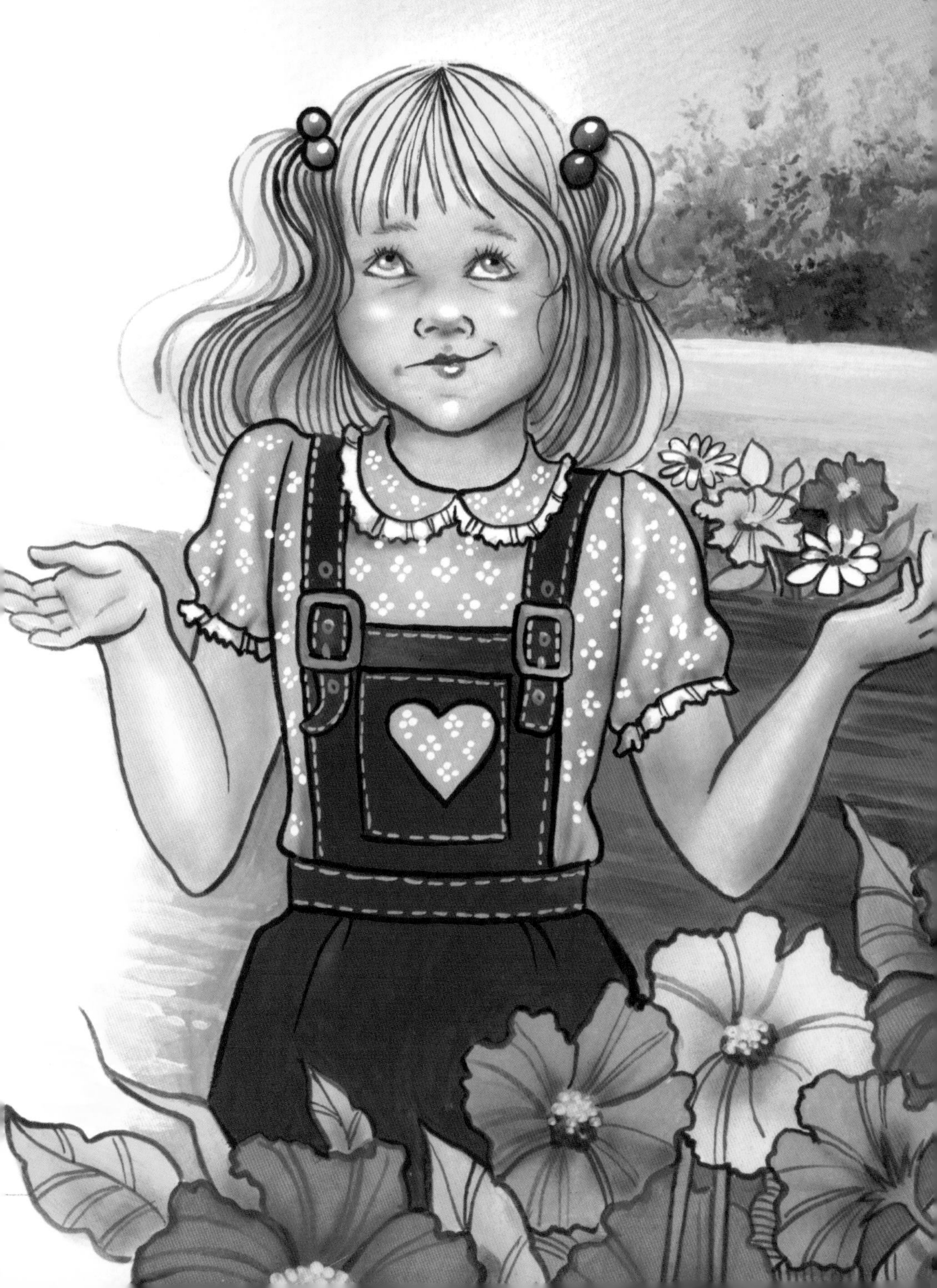

Then she spied it
right there at her feet!

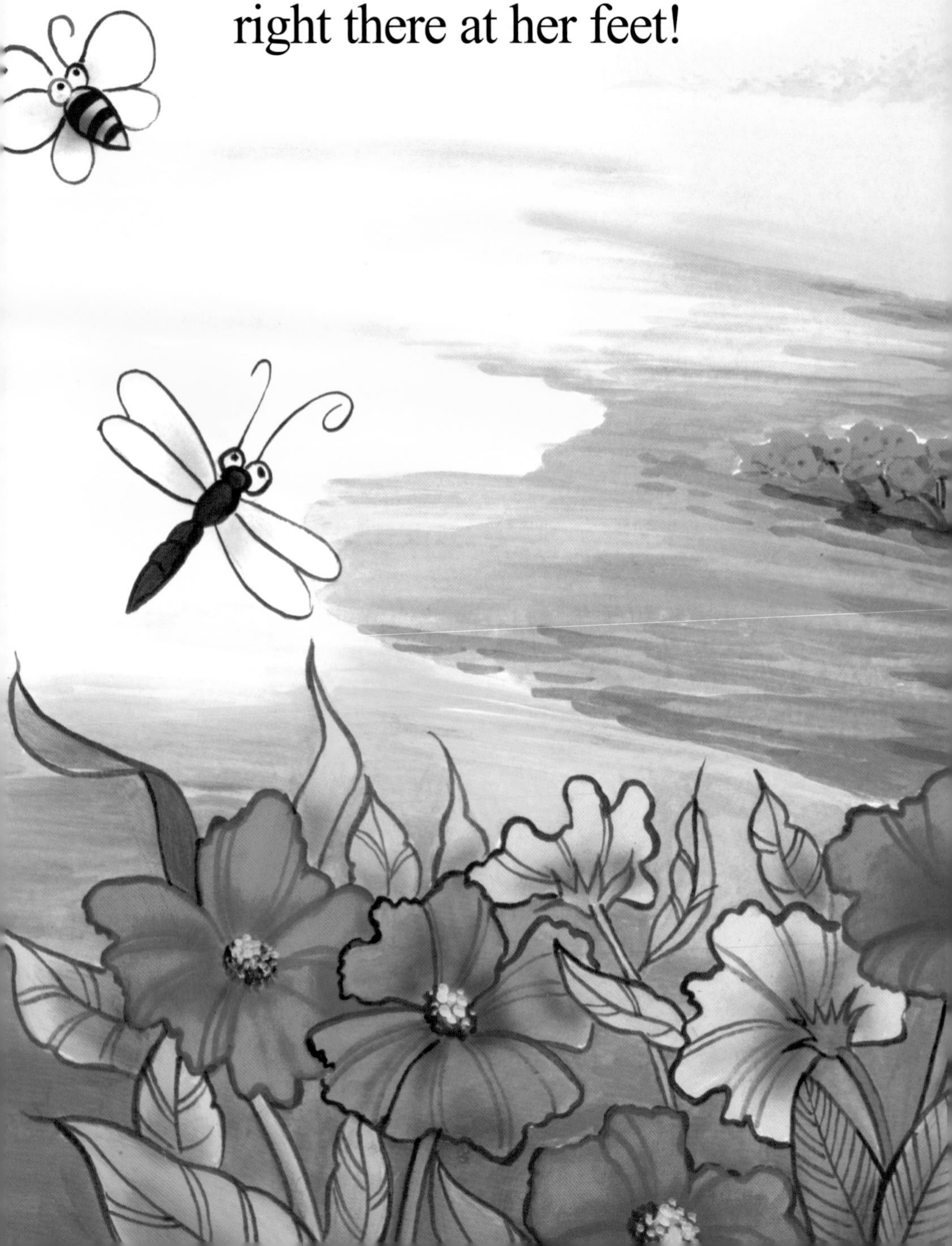

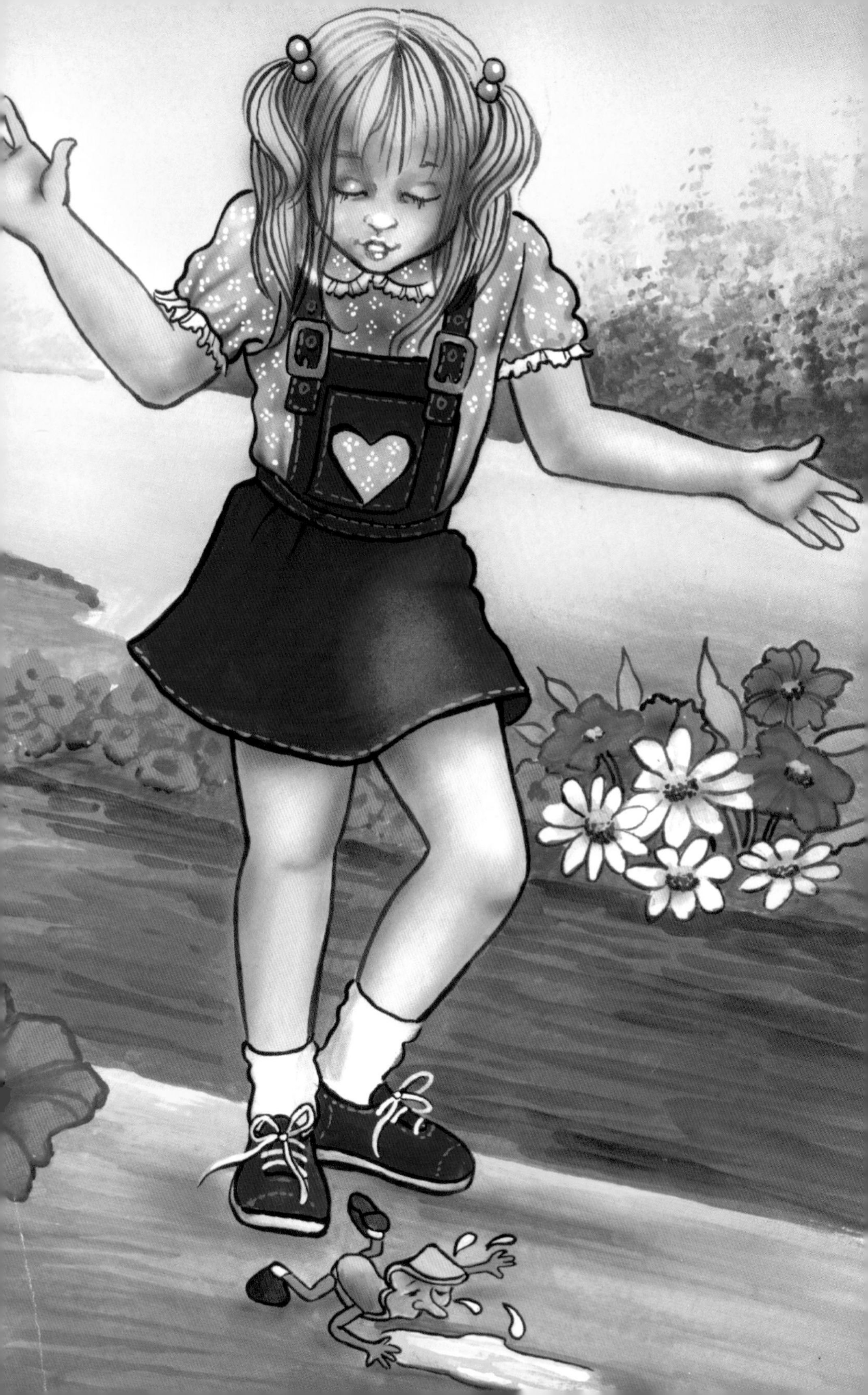

There at her feet, with tears all around, she saw the tiniest speckle.

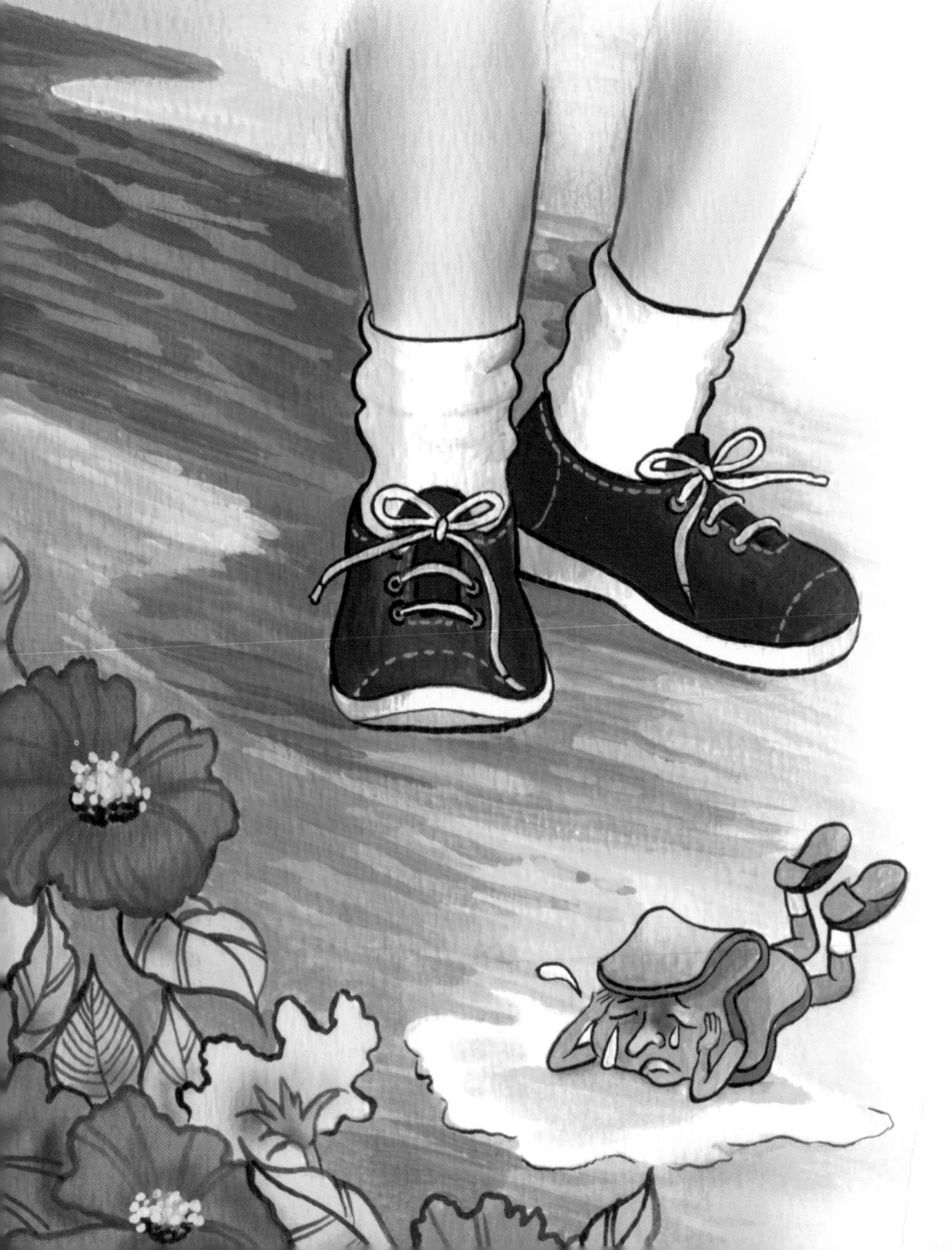

She bent lower,
close to the
ground...

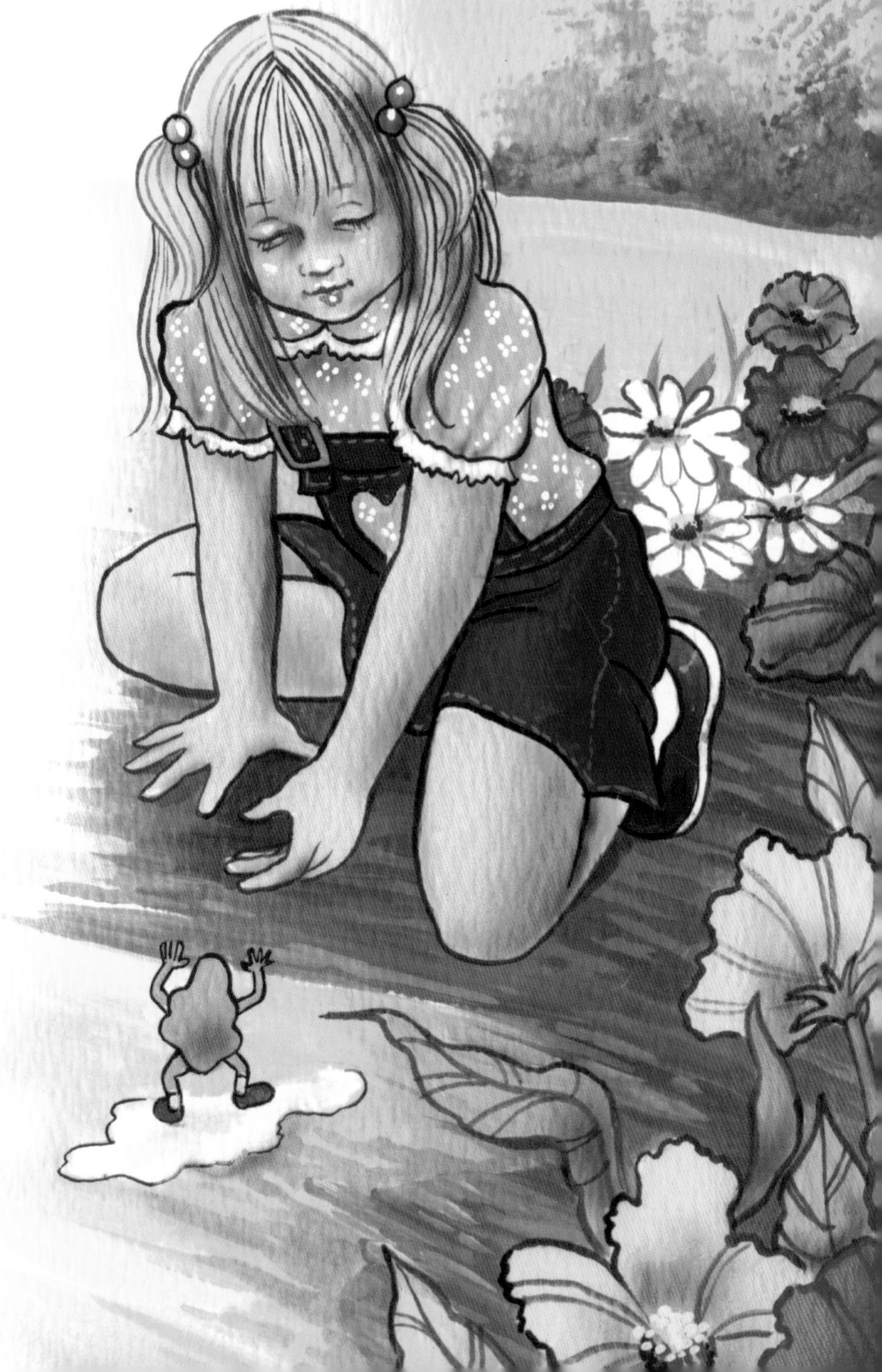

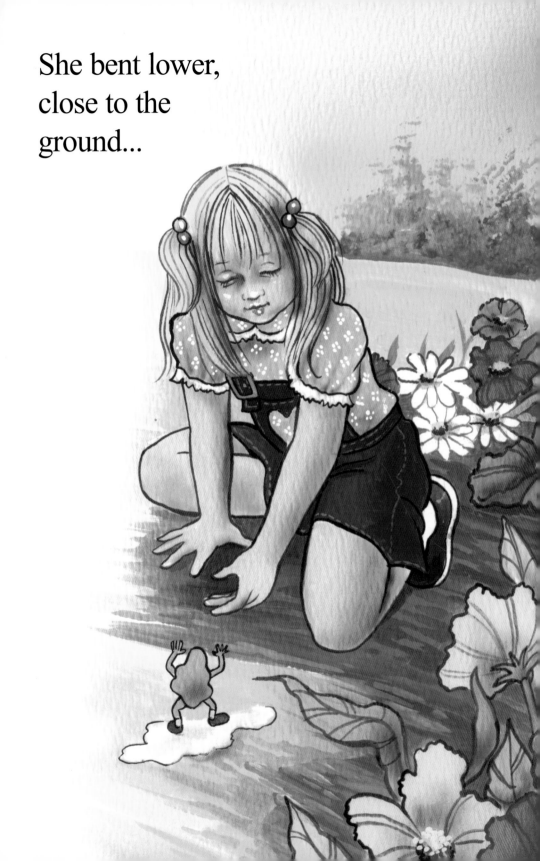

AND BEHOLD!

There was
Freddie Q. Freckle!

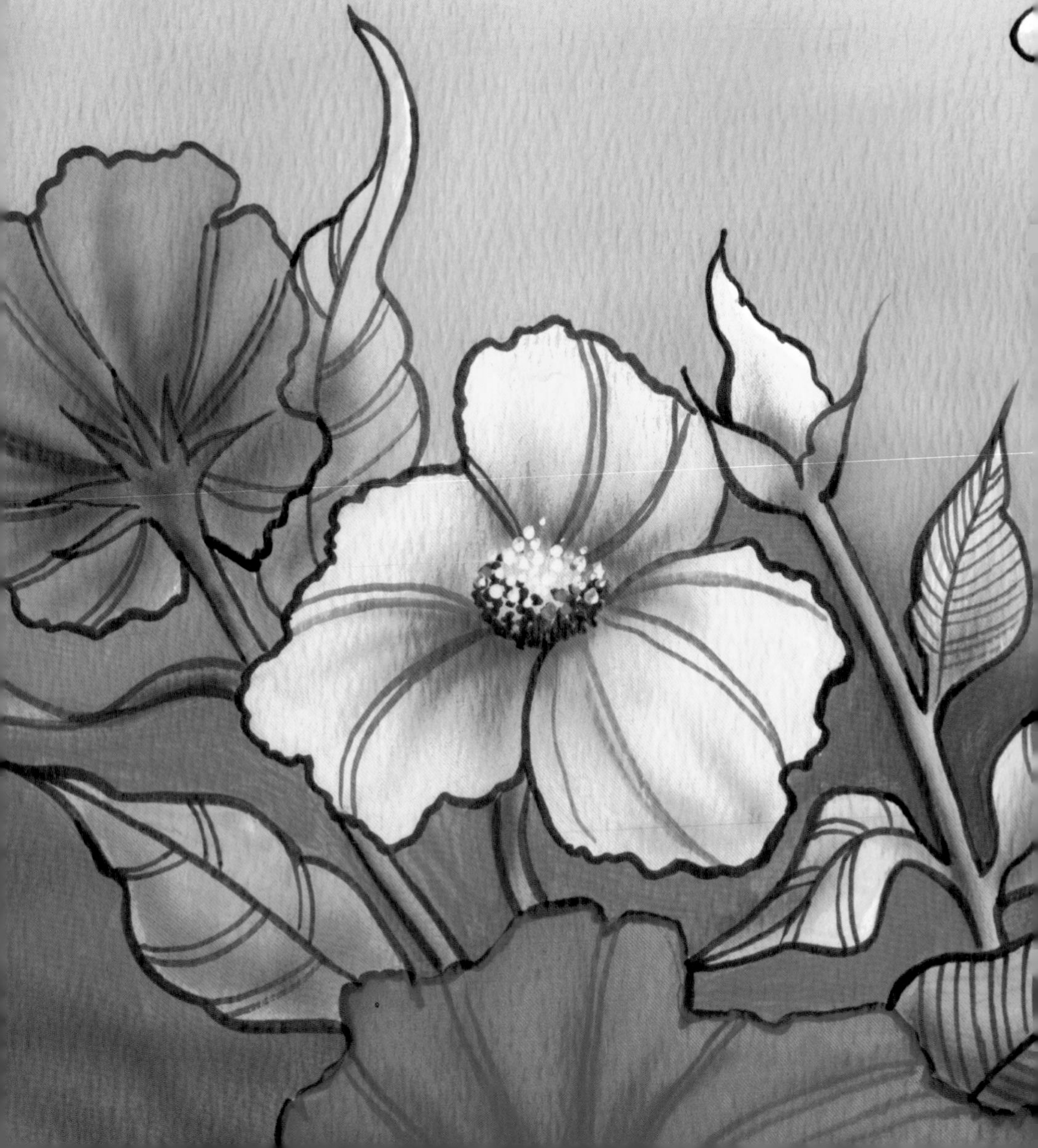

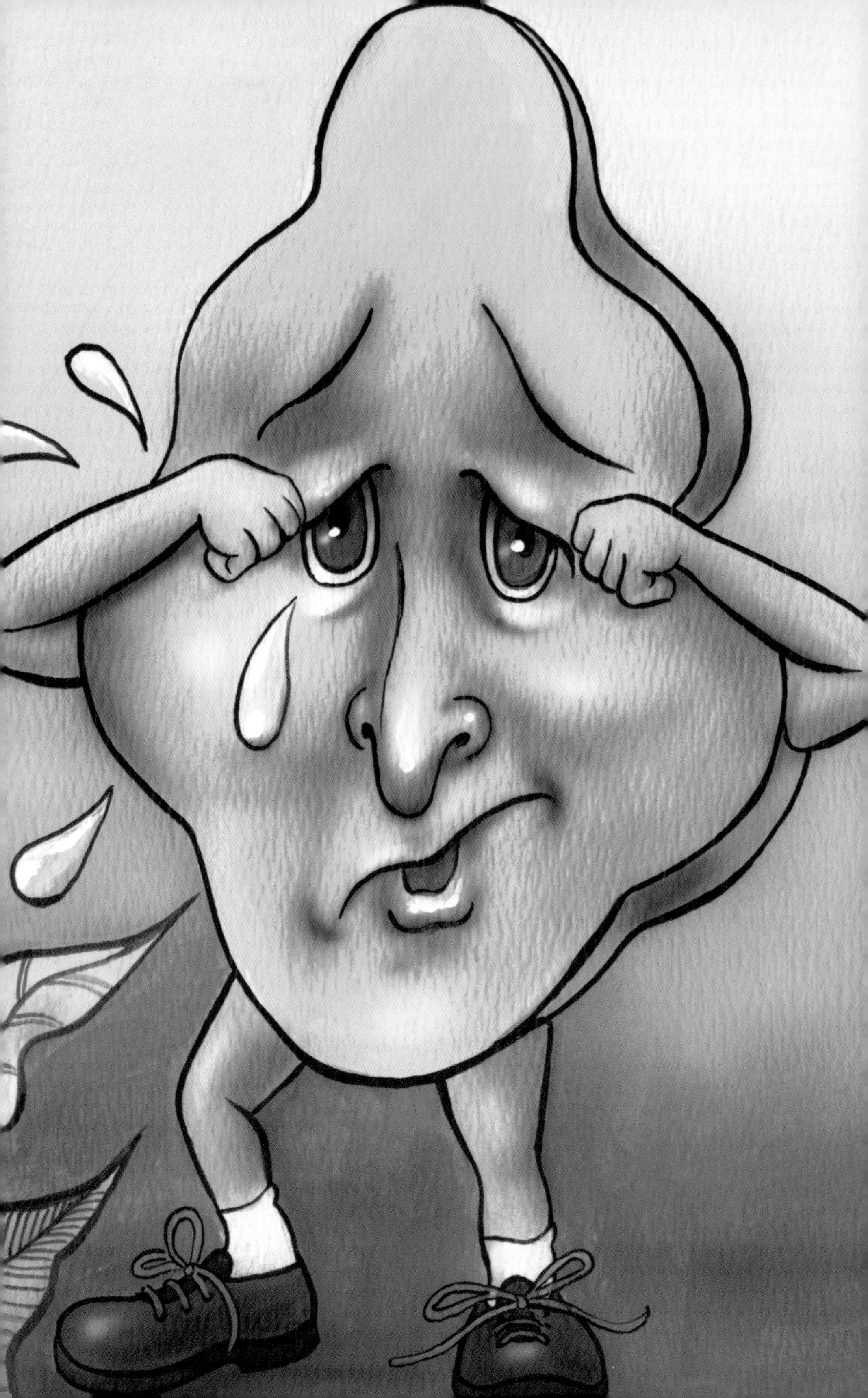

"Why are you crying, you sweet little thing? Why are you so sad and so blue?

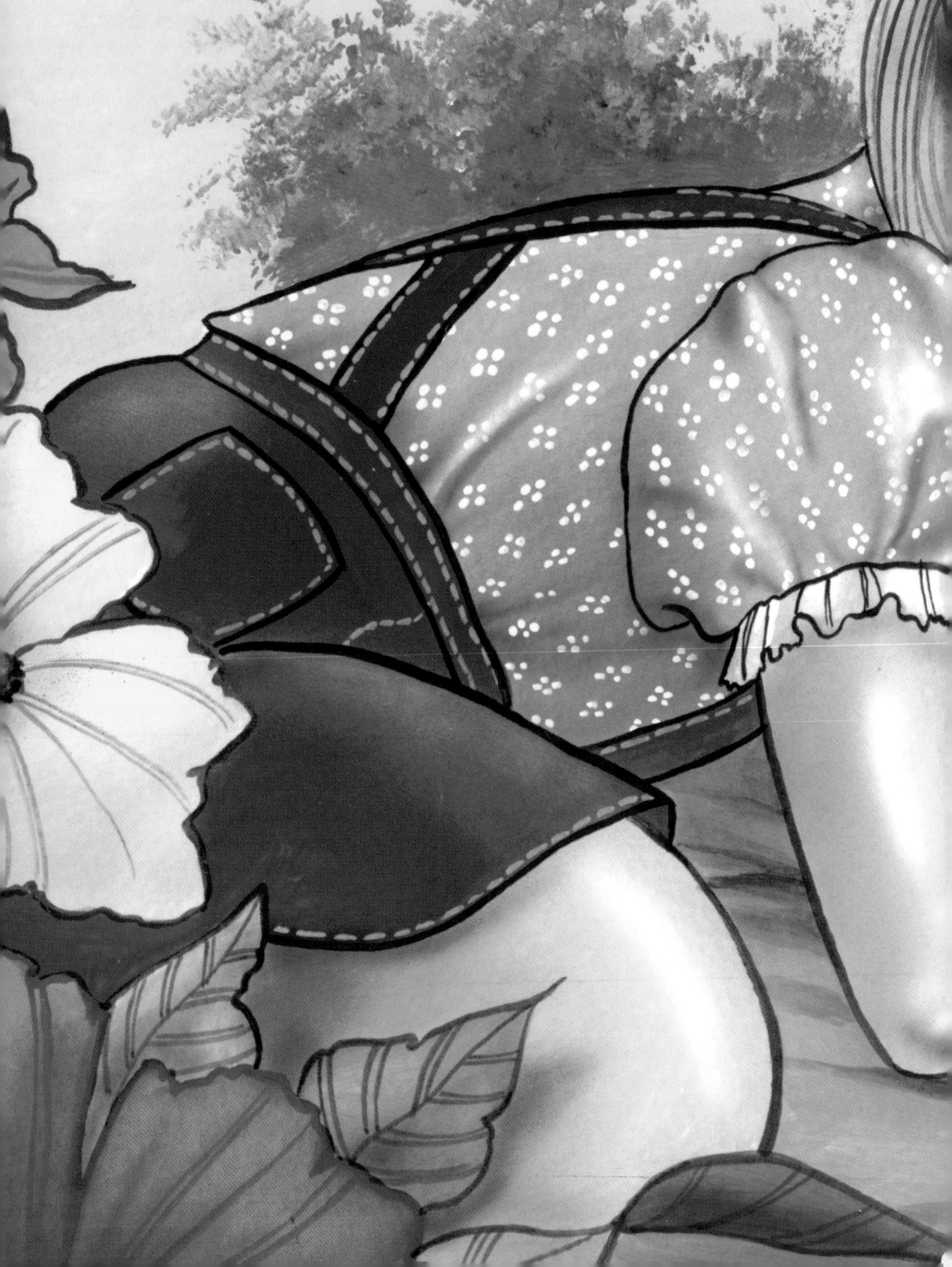

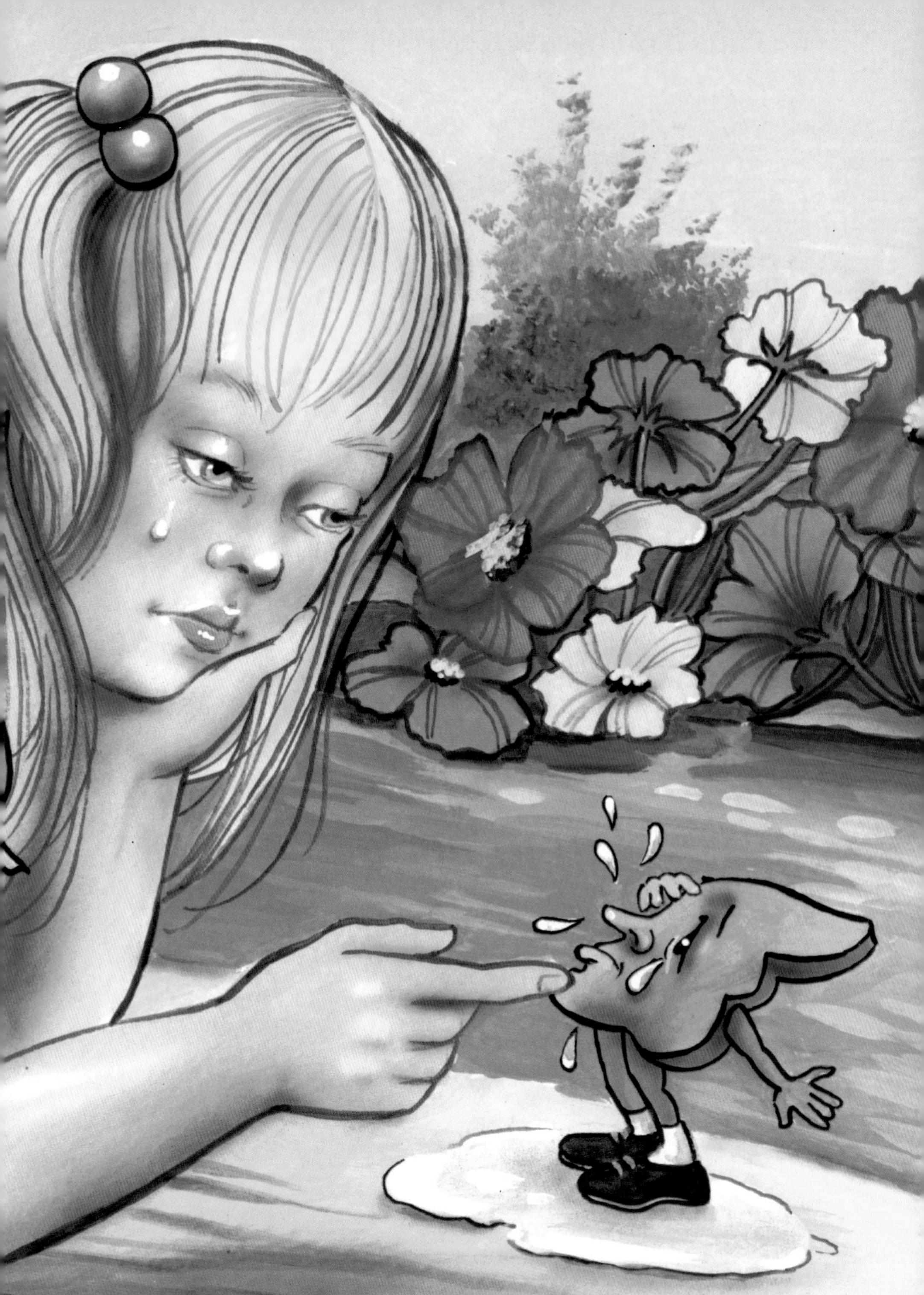

Won't you tell me if there
is anything that I'm able to do for you?"

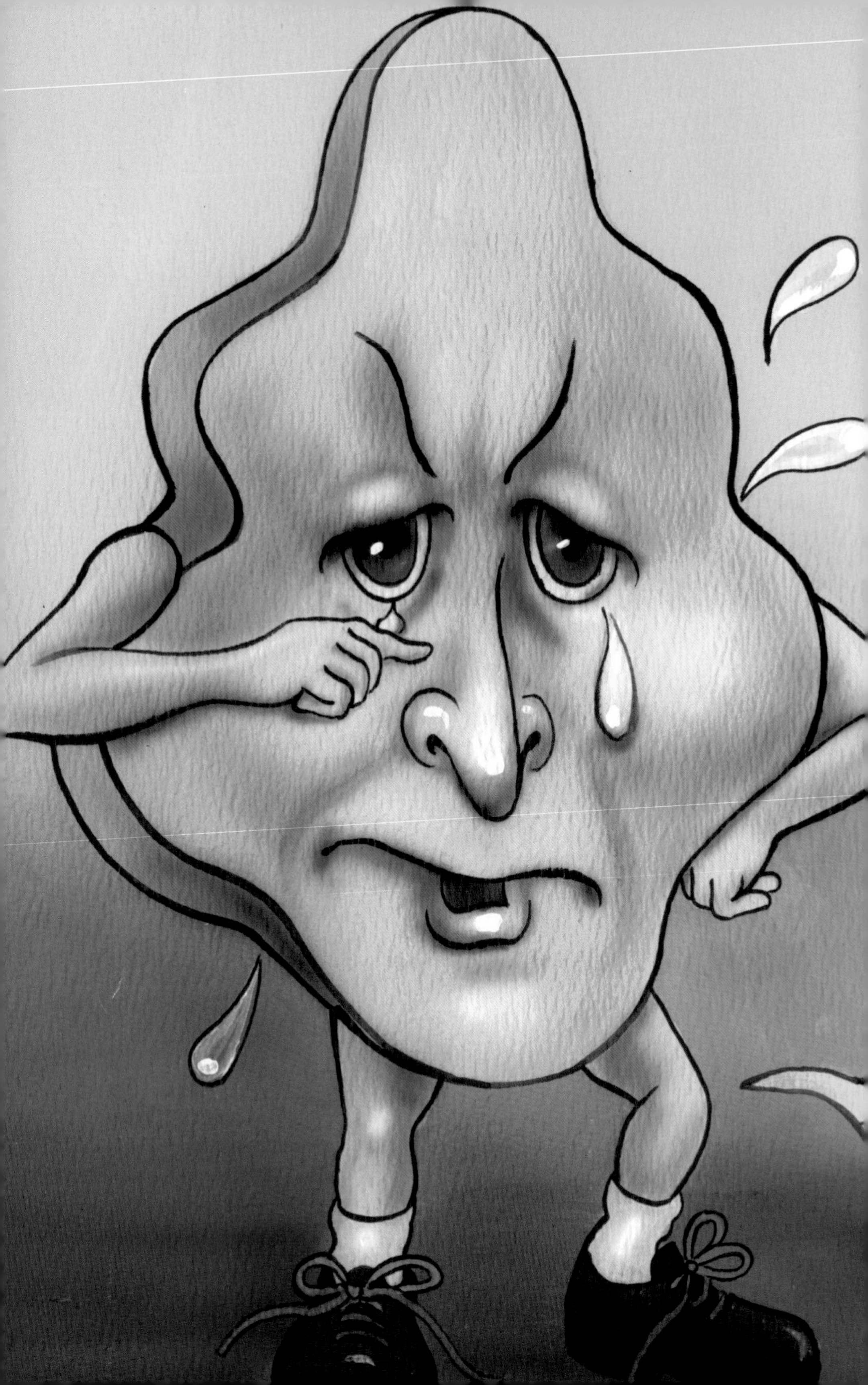

*"I cry, little girl,*
*for I'm very sad...*
*I've looked and looked,*
*but there's no home to be had."*

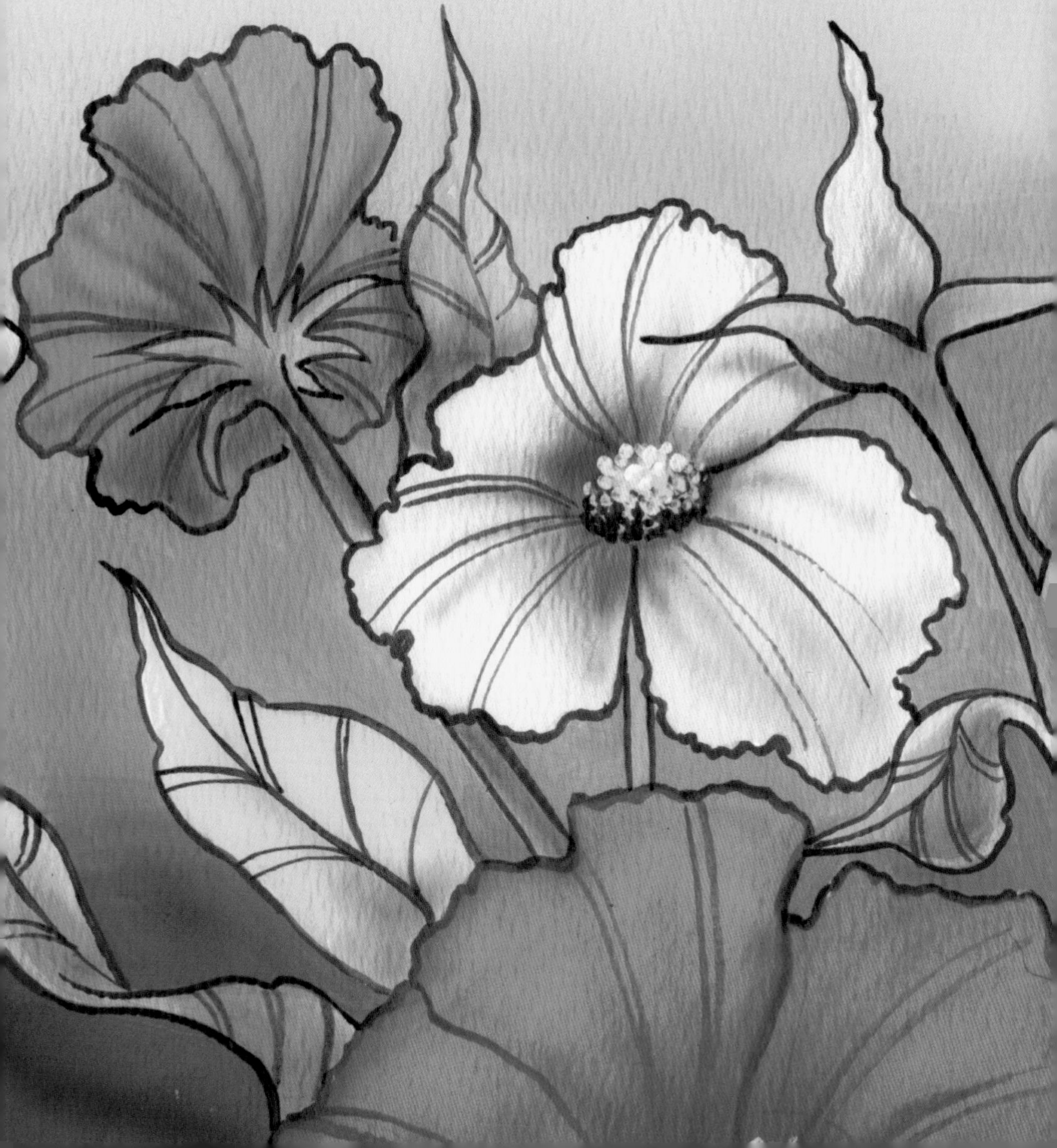

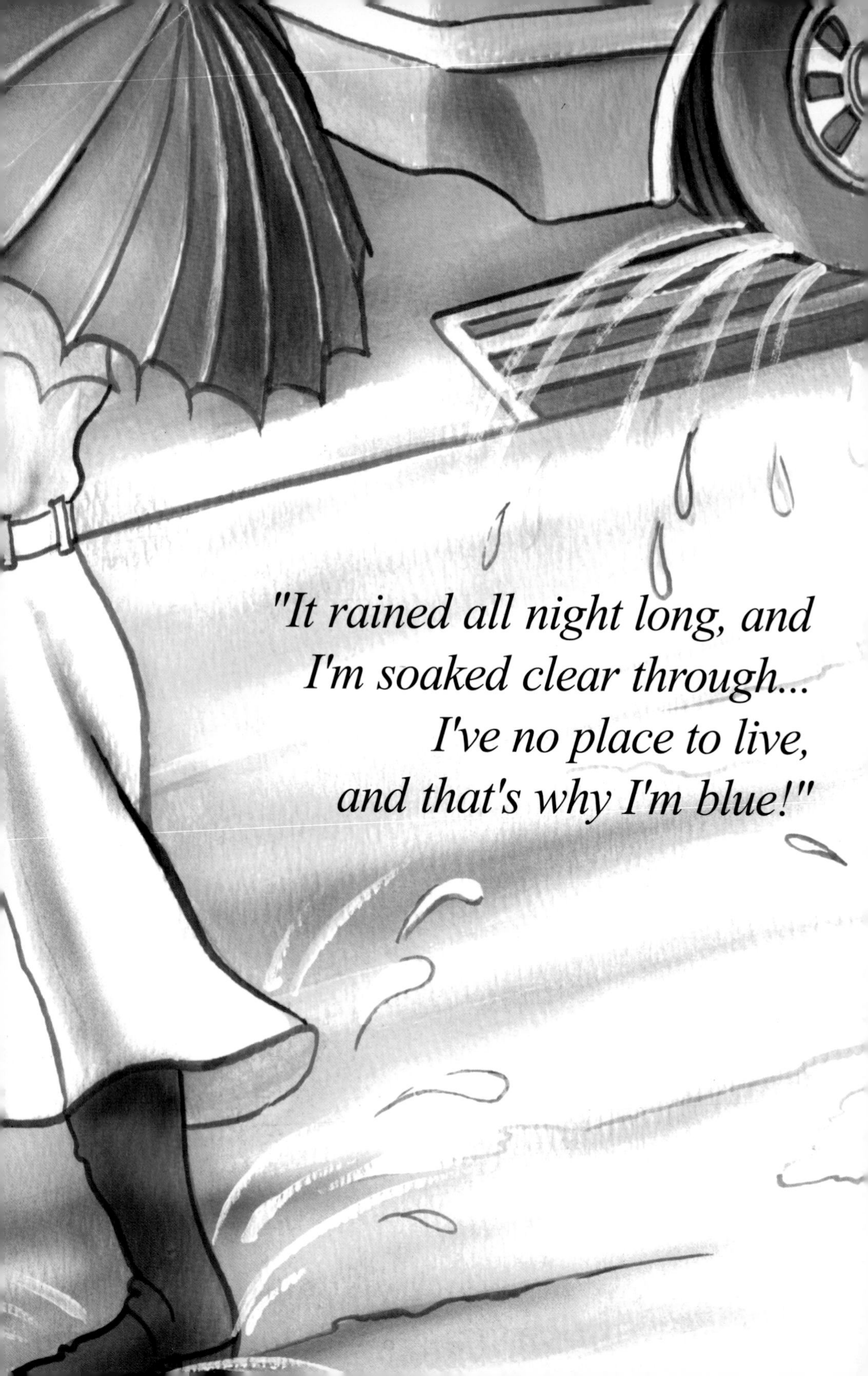

*"It rained all night long, and*
*I'm soaked clear through...*
*I've no place to live,*
*and that's why I'm blue!"*

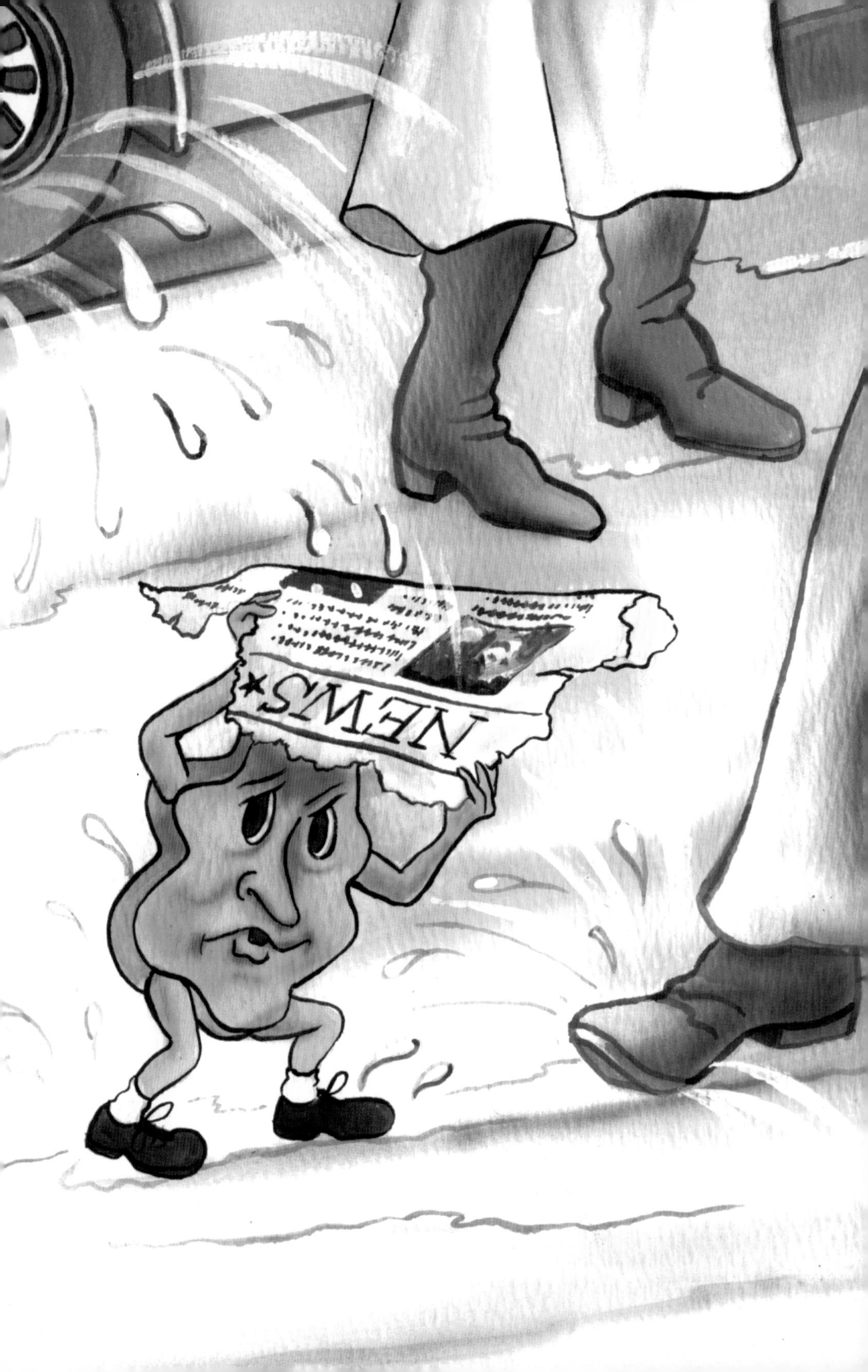
NEWS

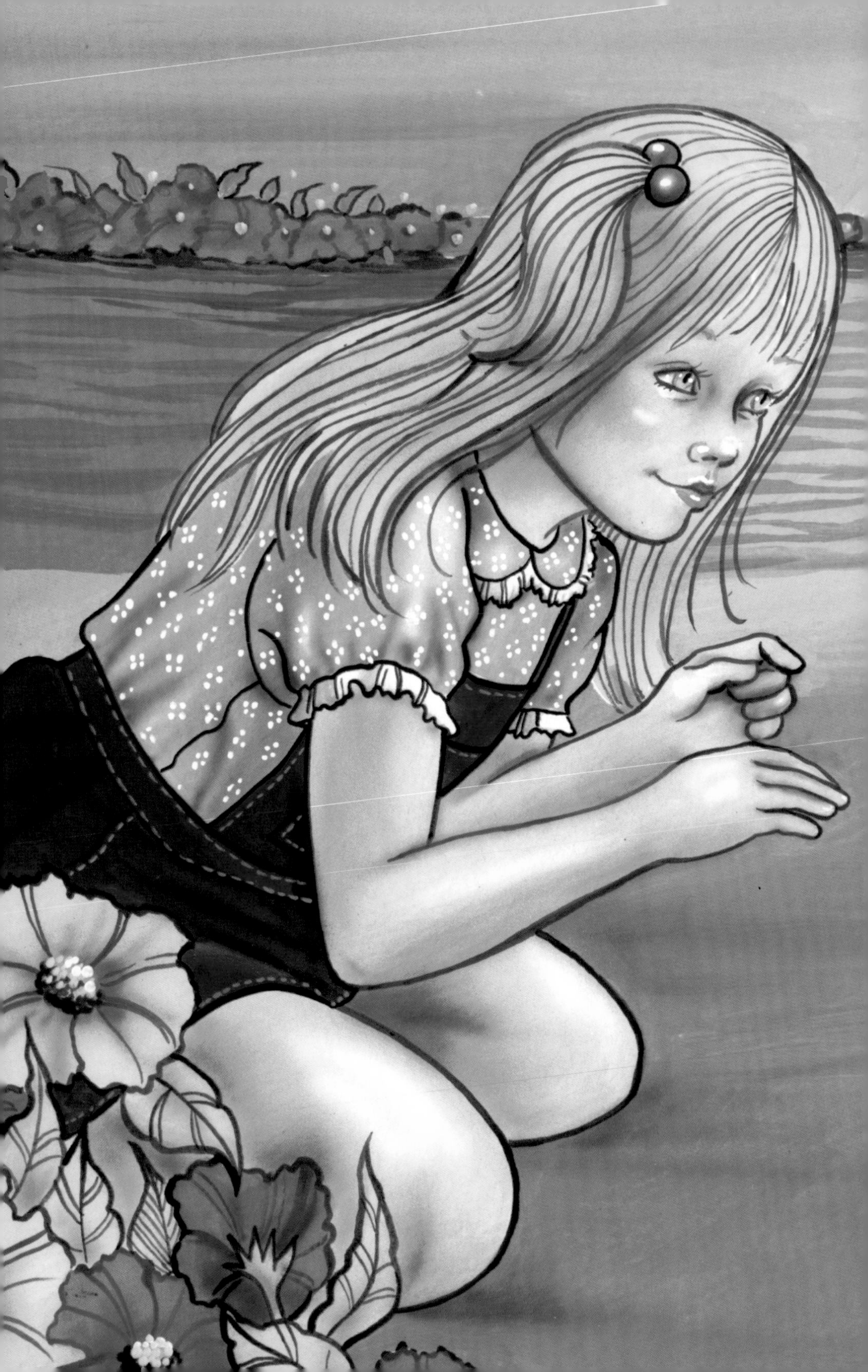

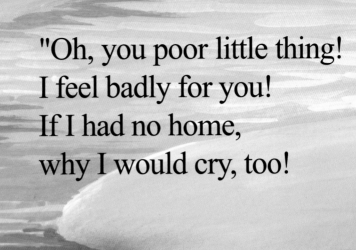

"Oh, you poor little thing!
I feel badly for you!
If I had no home,
why I would cry, too!

But don't weep any more,
for it would be grand,
if you would care to live
right here on my hand!"

Now Susie had never
seen any place,
a smile such as Freddie Q.
had on his face!

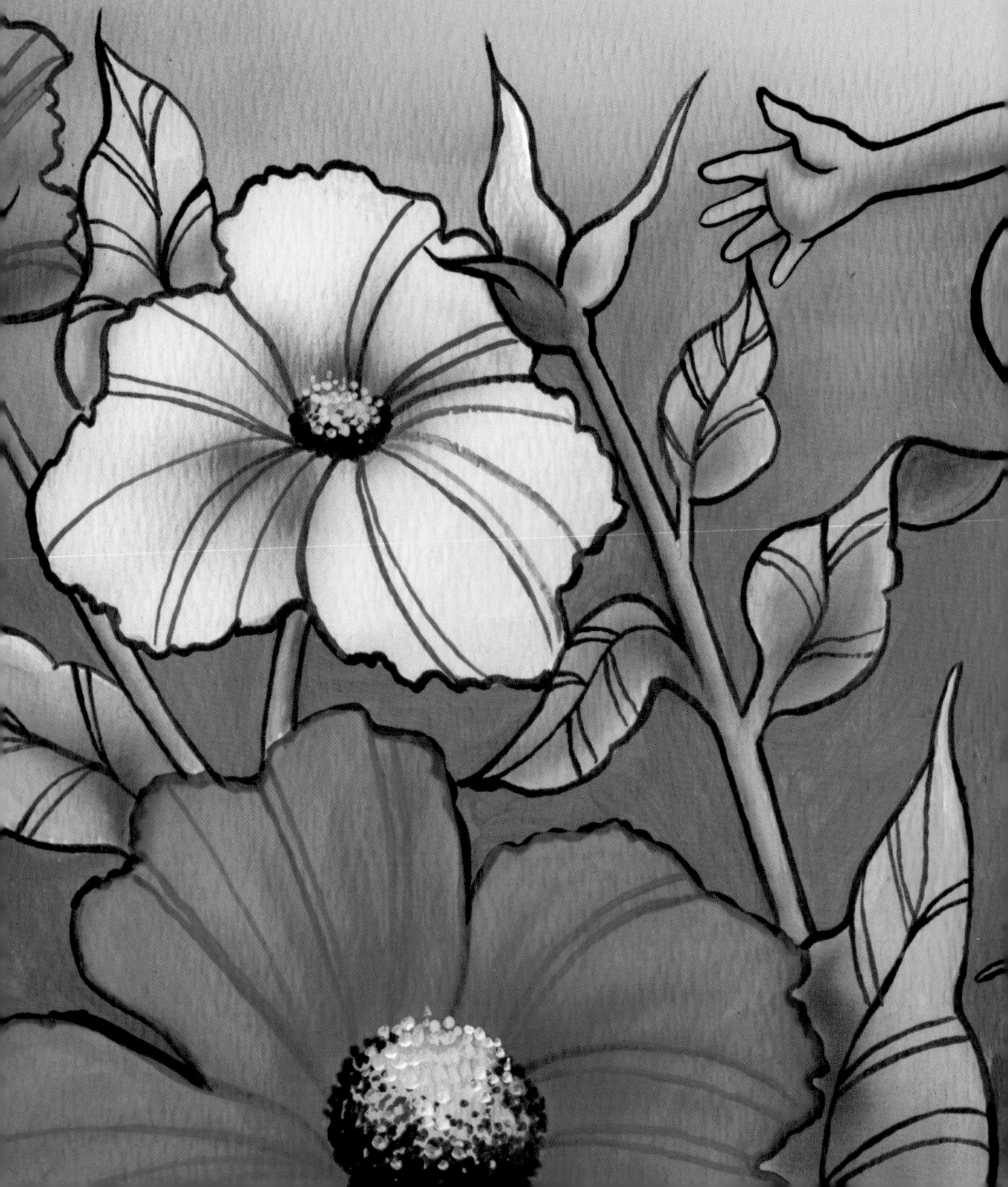

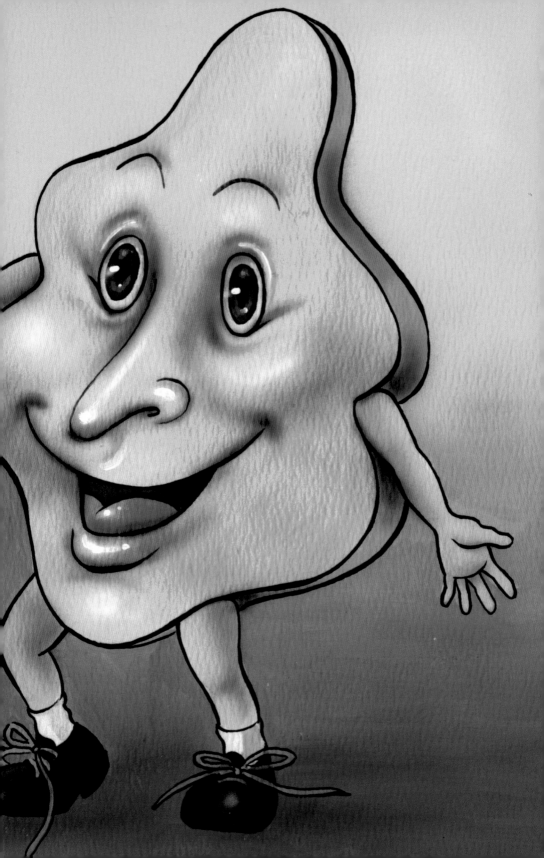

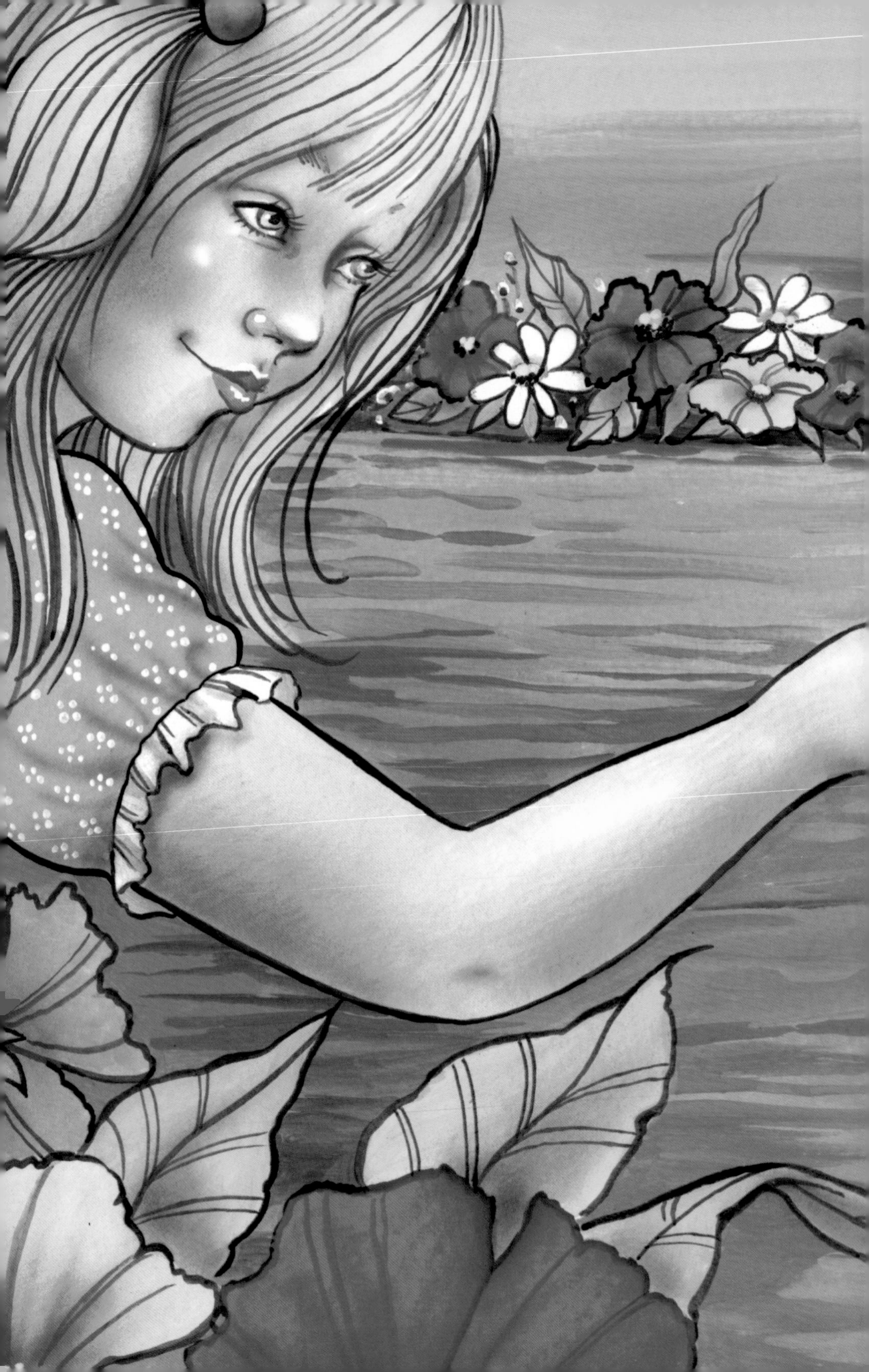

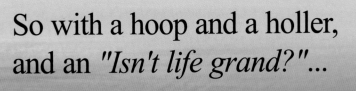

So with a hoop and a holler,
and an *"Isn't life grand?"*...

...With a leap and a bound,
he landed right on her hand.

So when
Susie awoke,
why, she was
so glad...

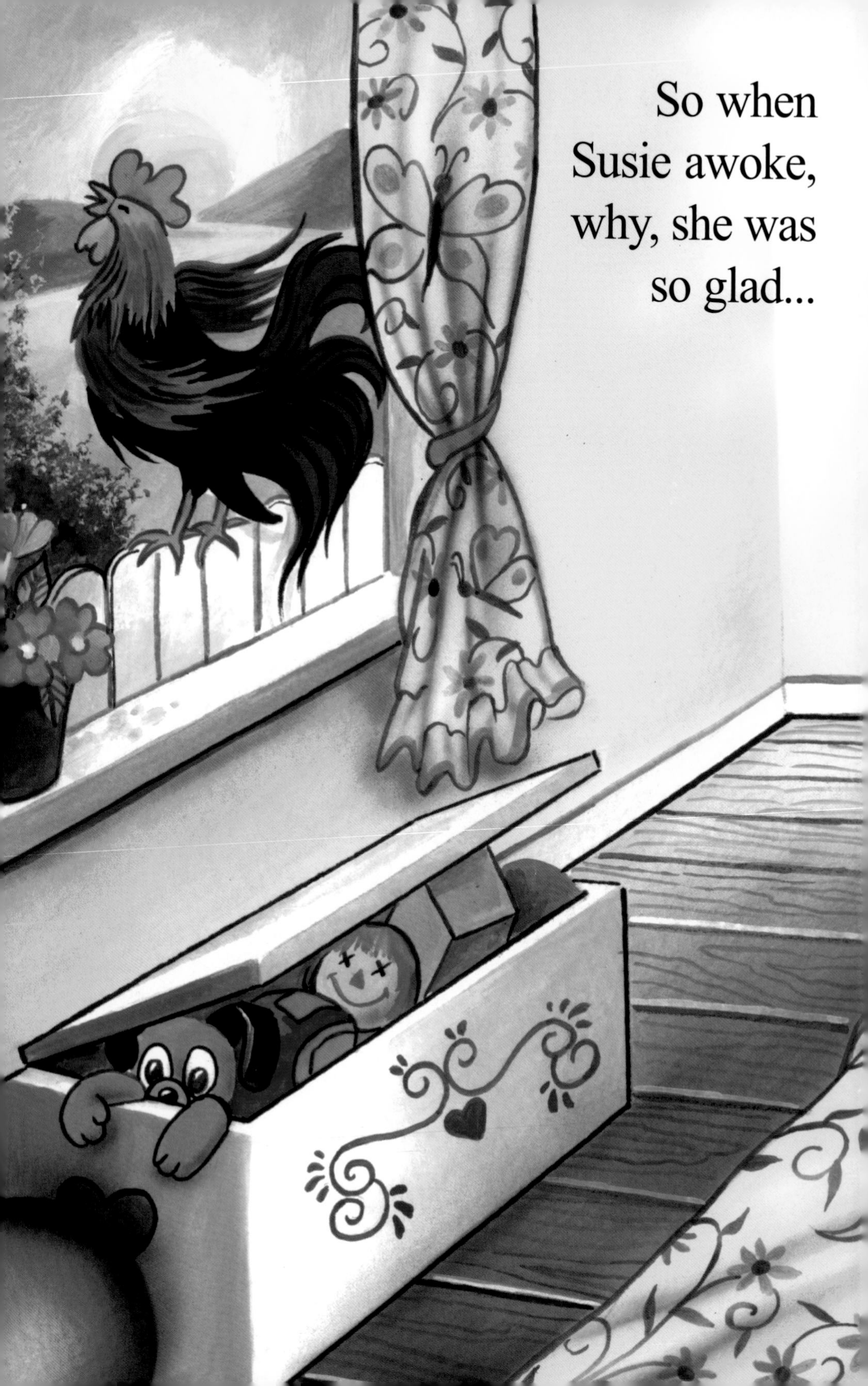

...because of the wonderful dream that she had.

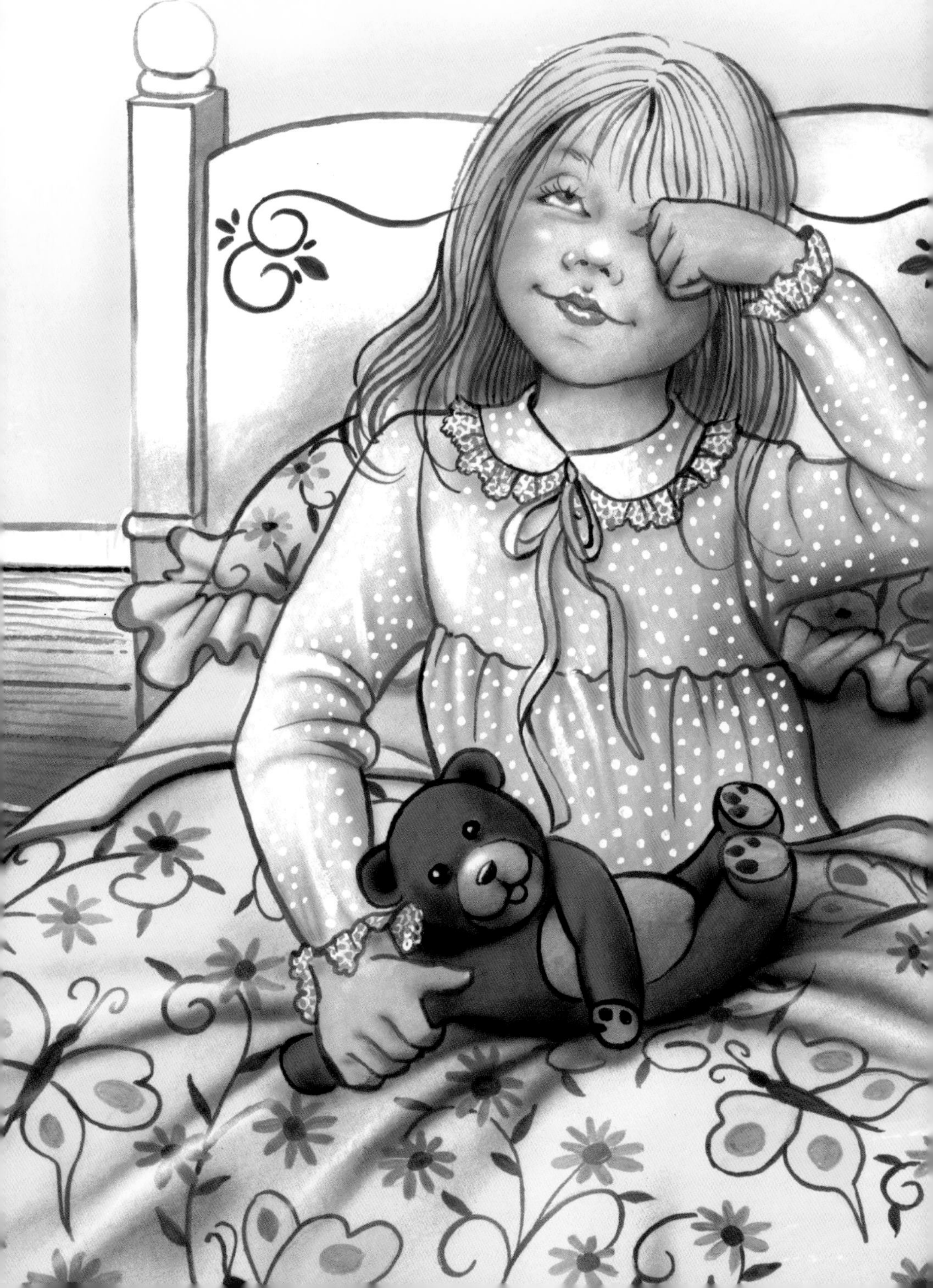

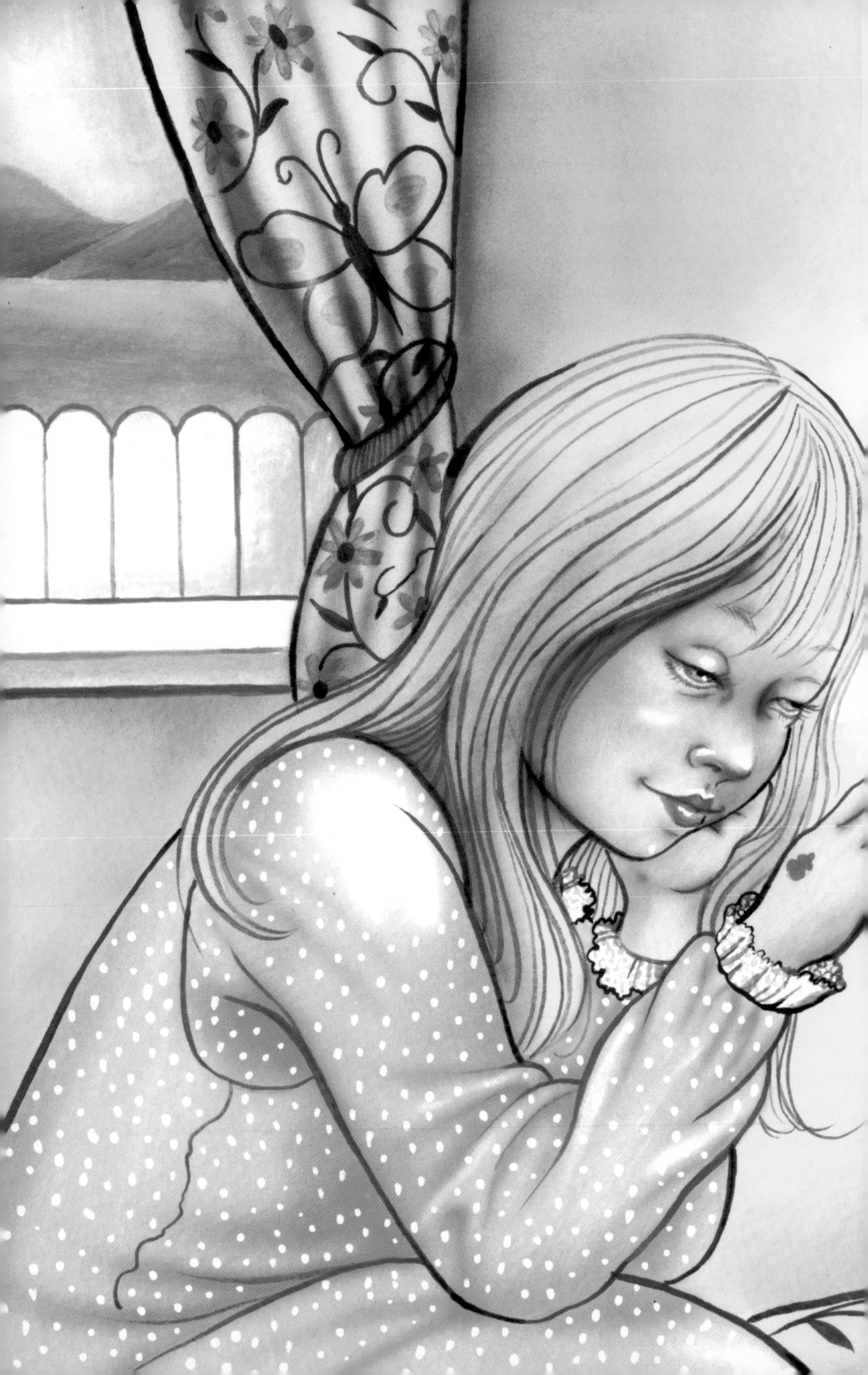

But when she looked at her hand,
she saw a tiny new speckle...

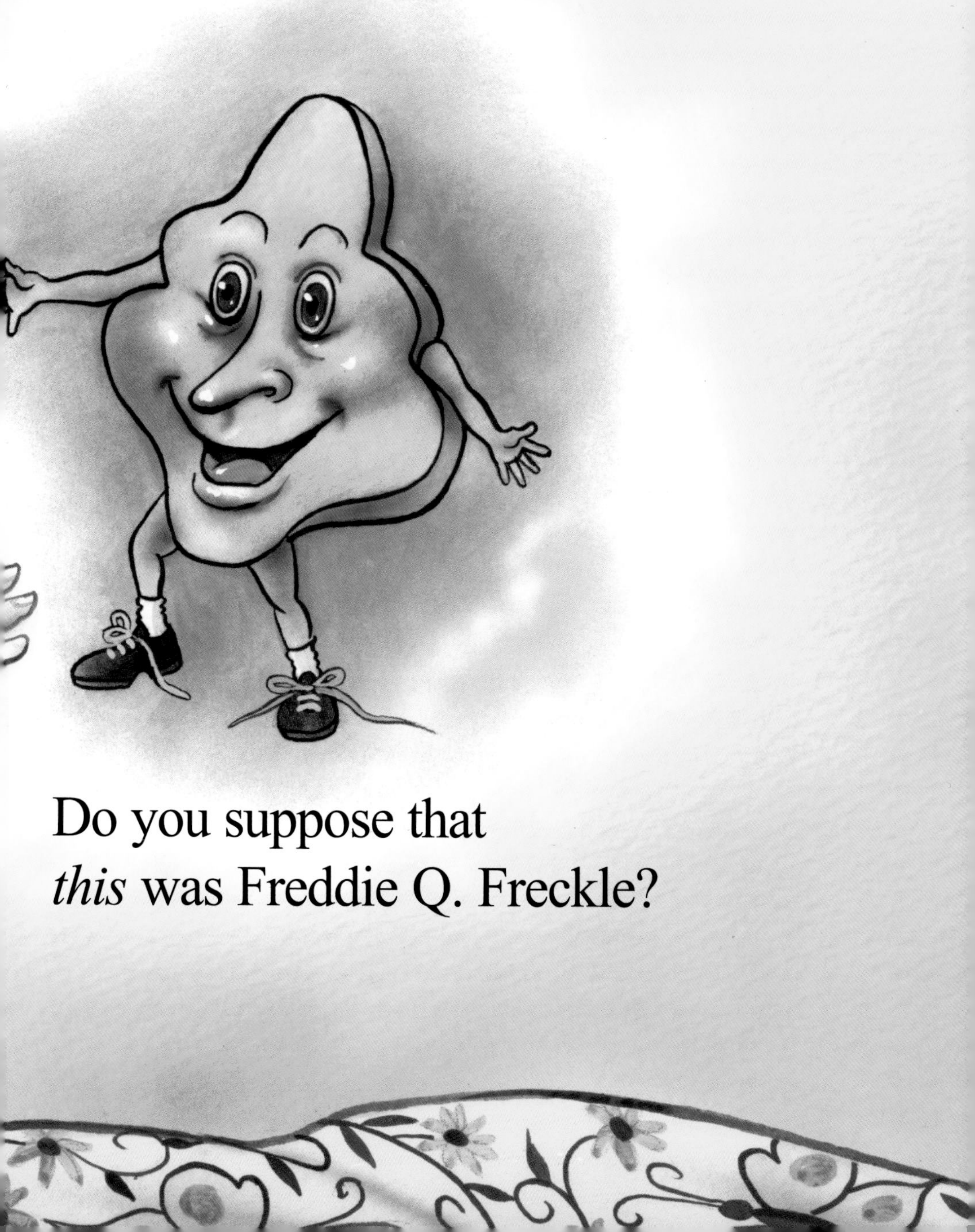

Do you suppose that
*this* was Freddie Q. Freckle?